The Clue in the Camera

Nancy led the way toward the nearby wharves. She slowed as she and George reached a row of little stores close to the waterfront. Suddenly Nancy touched George's arm, and the two came to a halt. Directly ahead of them was the man who had stolen Emily's camera two days before!

Without a word, the girls began pursuing the thief. Moments later, two other men emerged from a doorway in front of the girls. They, too, moved down the street, behind the man.

The girls watched as the two men crossed the street to a pay telephone. Nancy and George darted through an alley, stopping just where they could overhear the phone conversation.

Nancy leaned forward, straining to catch the conversation. The words she heard were chilling. "Lost him . . . Silence someone . . . before it's too late!"

Nancy Drew Mystery Stories

Available from MINSTREL Books

NANCY DREW MYSTERY STORIES®

82

NANCY DREW®

THE CLUE IN THE CAMERA

CAROLYN KEENE

A MINSTREL® BOOK

PUBLISHED BY POCKET BOOKS

New York   London   Toronto   Sydney   Tokyo

A MINSTREL PAPERBACK *ORIGINAL*

 A Minstrel Book, published by
POCKET BOOKS, a division of Simon & Schuster, Inc.
1230 Avenue of the Americas, New York, NY 10020

ISBN: 0-671-64962-0

Produced by Mega-Books of New York, Inc.

First Minstrel Books Printing March 1988

10 9 8 7 6 5 4 3 2 1

Contents

THE CLUE
IN THE CAMERA

1

Mugging

Nancy Drew looked out the window of the airplane. She nudged George Fayne, who was sitting next to her. "Look, George! The Golden Gate Bridge!"

George grinned. "A whole week in San Francisco. I can't wait!" she exclaimed.

Nancy Drew, her friend George, and Hannah Gruen, the Drews' housekeeper, were flying to the city by the bay to spend a spring vacation with Hannah's close friend Emily Foxworth, a famous photojournalist.

"Ladies and gentlemen." The captain's voice came over the plane's public-address system. "We are beginning our descent into San Francisco and will be landing shortly. Please fasten your seat belts."

Hannah Gruen straightened her skirt and ran her fingers through her hair. "I can't wait to see Emily. It's been so long!" Hannah and Emily had grown up together. They kept in touch by phone, but they didn't get to see each other often.

Hannah Gruen had taken care of Nancy and her father, attorney Carson Drew, ever since Nancy's mother had died years before. In that time, she'd rarely taken a vacation. But she'd been planning this trip to visit her old friend for a long time. Nancy's blue eyes shone as she watched Hannah primping in expectation of seeing Emily again.

The plane landed smoothly. Nancy, George, and Hannah unbuckled their seat belts and followed the other passengers off the plane and into the airport. Nancy was fumbling with her heavy jacket and her carry-on suitcase when Hannah exclaimed, "There she is!" and darted forward. Nancy and George grinned as Hannah embraced a trim, attractive older woman. Then Hannah turned and introduced the girls to Emily Foxworth.

"Welcome to San Francisco!" exclaimed Emily, shaking hands with each of them. "Think of me as your tour guide for the week. I plan to show you San Francisco from top to bottom. Well, you know what I mean!"

Nancy instantly liked Emily. "That sounds great," she replied, returning Emily's warm, genuine smile.

"How about a picture of the three of you?" suggested Emily. "I was thinking that I'd make a photo essay about your week in San Francisco. And it should begin here, at the airport."

"What a wonderful idea," agreed Hannah as Emily nudged them together and held up the professional-looking camera that hung from a strap around her neck.

"One, two, three. Smile!" said Emily. The three of them grinned. "Uh-oh! I'm out of film. Wouldn't you know it?" Emily explained that she had just come from shooting pictures in Chinatown. She was working on a photo assignment called "Children of Change" about young people growing up in large cities. "I run out of film at the most inconvenient times," she added. She opened the back of her camera, took out the exposed film, and handed the roll to Nancy to hold for her. Nancy dropped it in the pocket of her jacket.

"You won't have much need for those heavy coats you dragged along," Emily said while she reloaded the camera. "The weather's been gorgeous here." She grinned and snapped the camera shut. "Okay, let's try again. Say cheese."

Emily clicked off several pictures while Nancy, George, and Hannah smiled self-consciously. "Okay," Emily said, lowering her camera. "I'll get a few shots of you claiming your luggage. Then we'll take a taxi into town."

On the ride north into the city, Nancy sat in

3

the front seat beside the driver. She listened intently as Emily pointed out the sights along the way.

When the taxi stopped at a traffic light, Emily leaned forward. "For years now, Nancy," she said, "Hannah has been writing to me about your detective work. Finally, I've gotten to meet the famous teenage detective."

Hannah shook her head, but she was smiling fondly. "We all needed a rest from Nancy's latest exploit," she said. "So, for a week at least, we plan on forgetting all about solving mysteries."

"The most mysterious question we want to worry about in San Francisco is what famous restaurant to eat at each night," Nancy added, laughing.

"Well," replied Emily, "tonight the menu is Chinese. I plan on introducing you to San Francisco's Chinatown. I think you'll fall in love with it."

"Too bad Bess couldn't have joined us," George said. "I know she'd love it." Bess Marvin was George Fayne's cousin and Nancy's other best friend. She had planned to go on the trip but at the last minute had had to stay behind. "In fact," George continued, "she'd be complaining of hunger right now."

Hannah and Nancy smiled, recalling Bess's fondness for food. Her two main interests in life were eating and trying to lose five pounds.

"Okay," said Nancy. "Chinatown tonight. But

what about Ghirardelli Square and Fisherman's Wharf and the Golden Gate Bridge and the Japanese Tea Gardens and—"

Emily laughed. "Hold on! We'll have time for all of those things. First, let's get you settled in your hotel."

Nancy and George were both impressed by their first view of the elegant old hotel. "This place is huge!" George exclaimed as the cab pulled to a stop in front of it.

"Hundreds of rooms, and it's completely self-contained," Emily told them. "You can find anything you need right here within its walls."

A bell captain in a burgundy uniform opened the door of the taxi and took charge of their baggage. Hannah stopped for a moment and just stared at the sights of downtown San Francisco. Unlike Nancy and George, Hannah had not traveled extensively. She preferred to spend her days in River Heights taking care of the Drew household.

In their room, Nancy and George unpacked their bags. Through the open door to Hannah's adjoining room, they heard room service bringing the tea Hannah had ordered when they checked in. Hannah and Emily were still talking about how good it was to see each other again.

"I brought some new cassettes," George said excitedly to Nancy. "We can stay up all night if we want, listening to music. Isn't that what vacation is all about? Relaxing?"

"That's not my idea of relaxing, girls," Hannah called. "But you two go ahead and enjoy. I'll be sleeping next door. That's *my* idea of relaxing."

Nancy hung the last of her things in the closet and walked toward Hannah's room. "So when do we get to hear all about your adventures?" she asked Emily.

George ran a hand through her tousled dark hair and followed Nancy. "And when do we get to see your photos?" she wanted to know.

"Well, I thought we'd do some sightseeing first," Emily replied. "Then maybe you'd like a sneak preview of my photo exhibition. It's on display at a local art gallery."

"That sounds great. When do we start?" George asked.

"Any time. I'm ready when you are."

"Well, let's go," said Nancy.

"Wait. Just let me change out of my traveling clothes and into something more comfortable," said Hannah.

"Good idea," Nancy and George said together. "We'll meet you in the lobby," Nancy added, knowing she and George would be quicker than Hannah.

Back in their room, Nancy quickly changed into designer jeans and a new sweater for her first day of sightseeing. George chose a baggy blue sweater and tailored black pants. Fifteen minutes later, they got off the elevator in the lobby.

"This place is wonderful," Nancy commented,

looking up at the painted ceiling and the massive granite pillars supporting the second story.

George looked up, too, more dubiously. "It's wonderful as long as an earthquake doesn't strike. That cherub looks great up there, but I wouldn't want him sitting on my head."

Nancy laughed.

"Ready, girls?" asked Hannah, coming up to them. She looked as excited as a kid at a circus.

"You bet we are," Nancy replied.

"Let me get a picture," said Emily, and Nancy groaned inwardly. How much posing will we have to do this week? she wondered.

"Come stand in front of the hotel," Emily went on. Just as she was preparing to snap the shot, a bald man dressed in tennis shoes, jeans, and an old sweatshirt rounded the corner, ran toward Emily, and jerked the camera out of her hands.

"Hey!" cried Emily. "Stop him!" She made a grab for the thief. He slowed down only long enough to give her a shove.

Emily Foxworth slumped to the pavement.

2

A Face in the Mob

When Nancy saw Hannah help Emily to her feet and knew that Emily wasn't hurt, she searched the crowded sidewalk for the bald man. At last she spotted him rushing across an intersection, Emily's camera clutched against his side like a football.

"You stay there!" she shouted to George, Emily, and Hannah. Then she tossed her shoulder bag to George and ran after the man.

She was able to keep him in sight for about a block. He raced up a steep hill against a crush of businesspeople and tourists. But as she reached the top of the hill, Nancy got her first glimpse of the twists in the road. Ordinarily they were charming, she supposed, but right now they were a nuisance.

The thief was nowhere to be seen. He had rounded a corner, and dozens of people blocked Nancy's view. She couldn't even guess which way to run.

Shaking her head, Nancy gave up and walked back to the others, who were waiting for her at the hotel. George and Hannah were looking anxiously at Emily, who had had the breath knocked out of her.

"I lost him, Emily. I'm sorry about your camera," Nancy said as she joined the three on the hotel steps. "Are you all right?"

"Of course I'm all right, Nancy. Just mad. I've run into much tougher guys than that punk." Emily dusted herself off. George winked at Nancy and nodded that all was well as she returned her friend's shoulder bag.

"I think we're just a little shaken up," George said.

"Well, that won't do for my guests." Emily Foxworth snorted. "This is your vacation, and I won't have it spoiled for you. Don't worry about my camera," she told Nancy. "Or about me. I'll tell my friend Lieutenant Chin about it, and I'm sure things will work out fine."

Emily led her guests down the street in the direction opposite from the one the thief had taken. Nancy linked arms with Hannah as they started down the hill.

Emily set a brisk pace, and they soon reached police headquarters. They entered, and, without

9

pausing, Emily walked straight to a door marked "Lieutenant Donald Chin." She knocked and opened the door.

"Hello, Don. How's it going?" she asked.

A smile lit up the police officer's face when he saw Emily. Donald Chin, a trim Chinese-American who had served in the Downtown precinct for fifteen years, knew Emily and other journalists and newspeople well. He stood up to greet her and motioned the others to come in.

"Emily! We haven't seen much of you around here lately," he exclaimed. "I was wondering what sort of scheme we'd have to cook up to get you and your camera down here soon. Where *is* your camera?"

Emily shrugged sheepishly. "That's why I'm here. A thief made off with my best old camera just a little while ago."

Emily introduced Hannah, Nancy, and George and then described the incident to the lieutenant. He listened intently, showing concern when Emily told how Nancy had chased the thief.

"You ought to be more careful in a large city like San Francisco," he said sternly. "You might have been in a tight spot if you'd caught up with the thief."

"Nancy's a good detective, Don, with a lot of experience," Emily said.

"Perhaps," Lieutenant Chin said, but he didn't look convinced. "I doubt you'll ever see that camera again, Emily," he told her. "It's a good thing you have others."

Then the lieutenant produced a printed form and began filling in the information Emily gave in answer to his questions. Nancy supplied information about the thief's height, his balding but reddish hair, and his tan corduroy jacket. Lieutenant Chin looked keenly at Nancy and complimented her on her ability to observe and remember.

"See? I told you she was good!" Emily chuckled as she signed the report and pushed it across the desk to the detective. He smiled and agreed.

Then he looked at Emily, and his smile faded. "Have you been following the reports on the recent arrival of mob hoods and ringleaders in the city, Emily?" he asked gravely. "We're pretty puzzled by this sudden increase in underworld celebrity visitors. We're keeping a sharp watch to see what it means." Lieutenant Chin paused, then his smile flashed again. "With your reporter's mind," he teased, "I'm surprised you aren't already gathering hall-of-fame portraits of these mobsters."

Emily laughed. "I already have shots of most of the big guys from other assignments I've covered. That crime exposé I did a few years back provided me with pictures of just about everyone who's anyone in the world of crime. Besides, I'm off duty while Hannah and the girls are in town. I'm taking a real vacation."

11

After chatting with her friend for a few more minutes, Emily rose and said goodbye, and she and Nancy, George, and Hannah left.

When they got outside, Emily said brightly, "Now, let's try to have some fun."

"That sounds like a good plan to me," Hannah said. "And I have a suggestion."

Nancy smiled, happy to see Hannah enjoying her role as tourist.

"Even though it's only four o'clock in San Francisco," Hannah continued, "it's already six in River Heights. And my stomach is on River Heights time."

"Dinner?" Emily asked immediately. Nancy, George, and Hannah all nodded enthusiastically. "There's a BART station only a few blocks away," Emily said. "We could take that over to the Embarcadero."

George cocked an eyebrow at Nancy. They had planned to spend one afternoon using the Bay Area Rapid Transit—a sleek, fast train system—for some exploring on their own.

"But," Emily said, joining a group of tourists waiting at a corner, "for your first day in San Francisco, this will be more appropriate."

A bell clanged loudly, and one of San Francisco's famous cable cars crossed the intersection. Nancy watched Emily's face light up with pleasure as the handsome old car glided toward them on its web of overhead cables.

"A cable-car ride and dinner in Chinatown—

welcome to San Francisco!" Emily exclaimed as they waited to board.

"Will we ride this all the way to Chinatown?" Nancy asked.

"Most of the way. We'll get off at Bush Street and walk over to Grant Avenue. You'll see why," Emily added mysteriously.

There were three empty seats on the old cable car, and George, Hannah, and Emily took them. Nancy was happy to stand, holding on to a rail and gazing outside as they rode up and down the hills of the city. In the late-afternoon sunlight, everything seemed to have a golden glow.

A tourist on the street aimed a camera at the cable car. Nancy thought of Emily's camera and frowned. If Emily were just a tourist, Nancy thought, the loss of her camera wouldn't seem so bad. But Emily's camera was important to her. It was part of her life. Nancy was glad that the only shots on the film that had been in the camera were of her and George and Hannah.

As the cable car toiled up another hill, Emily signaled to Nancy and the others that they would get off at the next stop.

"I really enjoyed that," Hannah said as they walked toward Grant Avenue. "I'm beginning to feel like a world traveler." Nancy and George exchanged smiles.

"Nancy! Look!" George exclaimed as they turned onto Grant Avenue. She gestured ahead of her. Bright against the blue afternoon sky was a vivid green and ocher gateway decorated with dragons and stone lions.

"How lovely, Emily," Hannah said warmly as they walked through the gateway into China-town. "So that's why you took us this way."

Nancy and George walked slowly, looking all around. The pagoda rooftops, the street signs in Chinese calligraphy, the shops displaying exotic merchandise, the colorful silk clothing of some of the people on the crowded sidewalks all said that here was a piece of China, not just another neighborhood.

"What a setting!" George exclaimed. "I feel as if anything could happen here."

Even though Nancy had traveled more widely than George, she was just as excited as her friend at the prospect of adventure in this exotic setting. Solving mysteries in Paris, Java, and Venice had not dulled Nancy's pleasure in going to new places.

Emily led the little group through the crowded walkways. She pointed to a street sign that read "California Street" in Chinese characters and in English. "My favorite restaurant—Lee Chow's—is only a block away," she said.

Soon Hannah and the girls stood in the entry-way of a small restaurant, letting their eyes adjust to the dimness inside. The restaurant owner greeted Emily as an old friend and quickly led them to a table for four.

As soon as they had ordered, Nancy, who was

14

curious about Emily's knowledge of San Francisco and her friendships with its people, asked her to talk about some of her assignments.

"Oh, you're here to see the city, not listen to a speech about my work," Emily protested.

"Don't be modest," Hannah said with a smile. "I've told Nancy about your travels for years, and she's been looking forward to hearing everything firsthand."

After some prodding from George and Nancy, Emily agreed. She described some of her travels in Asia, where she had been one of the first woman photographers allowed entry to China when Western visitors were permitted again. After that, only a pause to pour tea or the arrival of their food interrupted Emily's stories.

"Hannah said you wrote a lot of crime stories and exposed some big-time crooks," Nancy said.

"I guess I've had my share of brushes with criminals. None of them ever stole my camera like that man today, though."

Everyone laughed. The encounter with the thief seemed far away from the cozy restaurant. Emily stopped to sip some tea before continuing.

"The criminal stories were a little like the 'Children of Change' story. I started taking pictures of something that interested me, and gradually I realized there was a story to be told, right in front of my eyes. Sometimes it was a matter of being in the right place to take a picture of a robbery, and before I could plan anything, another picture would present itself, another image, and soon I found myself covering a real story."

"Once," Hannah said, "I went to Chicago to meet Emily for a holiday weekend, and there had been an accident involving a commuter train. Emily disappeared for the rest of the weekend, doing research in city hall about the organization that provided maintenance for the trains. And she uncovered facts that proved who was at fault in the accident." Hannah laughed as she told them she had spent the weekend visiting museums and touring the city by herself, taking snapshots with her instant camera, while her friend worked night and day.

"It won't happen this time," Emily promised. "No work for me this week."

They finished their meal and left the restaurant. "Let's walk home," Emily suggested. "I've got dessert waiting for us."

Nancy, George, Hannah, and Emily strolled down Grant Avenue. They stopped often to look in the windows of curio shops, exclaiming over the gifts and making plans to return for more serious shopping.

Nancy enjoyed watching Hannah talk with Emily. They were practically like sisters, she realized, very different from each other, but very close. She could understand why Hannah had always spoken of Emily with respect and affection.

16

"Hey, let's send that to Bess," George said mischievously, pointing to a Chinese cookbook with a photograph of duck's feet on the cover.

Nancy laughed, then stopped as a reflection in the store window distracted her. She turned to study the crowd but saw nothing. She looked ahead and realized that Emily and Hannah were several paces in front of her and could easily be cut off by the busy crowd. George ran after Nancy when she moved quickly to catch up with the older women. "What's up?" she asked anxiously.

"I'm not sure yet, George. Keep your eyes open, okay?"

They had passed several more shops before Nancy could pin down what was bothering her. She thought there was something odd about the reflections she saw in the windows. Always Emily, Hannah, George, herself, and—that was it, someone else. Every time!

"I think we're being followed," Nancy said softly to George. She knew she could count on her friend to stay calm and be helpful. They continued to walk down the street with Hannah and Emily, pretending to be interested in the store windows. Soon Nancy was sure her hunch was correct; she always caught a glimpse of tan fabric in the reflections, or in the crowd when she glanced around.

Nancy had been careful to move at the same

17

pace as Hannah, Emily, and George, but after a few more steps, she stopped. She waited as the others walked away. Then she turned and looked directly into the crowd behind her—into the face of the balding, reddish-haired man who had stolen Emily's camera!

She knew he'd caught her looking at him.

3

Killing a Story

The man turned and disappeared into the bustling evening crowd of tourists and shoppers.

"Wait!" Nancy yelled. "Stop!" But he was gone.

"What is it?" Emily rushed to Nancy's side. Hannah and George crowded around, too.

"I saw him."

"Who?" asked Hannah.

"That bald man. I'm sure it was the guy who stole your camera, Emily. He wasn't totally bald. He had some hair. Red hair."

George let out a low whistle.

Emily frowned. "I remember seeing a man like that somewhere. I just can't remember where."

"Think, Emily," Nancy urged her. "I have a

feeling we're involved in something more complicated than a robbery. Why would that guy be following us? Try to remember where you've seen him before."

Emily furrowed her brow. "It's no good. I don't know where. But sooner or later it's bound to come to me."

Hannah looked worried. "Let's get out of here. I don't like this."

"We'll take a cab to my apartment," Emily told her. "Then we can relax for a while. Maybe I'll be able to remember where I've seen the mystery man."

"What about the photo exhibition? I wanted to see your photos, Emily," George said.

"There'll be plenty of time for that later," Emily answered. "I think we've had enough excitement for one day. Anyway, it's late. You three must be tired."

They continued down Grant Avenue until Hannah caught sight of a taxicab. She stepped off the curb. "Taxi!" she cried, waving to the driver.

Before the cabbie could pull over, two speeding cars turned a corner. With a squeal of tires, they headed straight for Hannah! Nancy grabbed her and pulled her out of the street just as a small foreign car followed by a black limousine whipped by and quickly disappeared.

"Hannah! Are you all right?" Nancy took her by the elbow and led her to a bus stop, where Hannah sat shakily on the bench.

"I'm all right," Hannah replied after a few moments. "Just a little scared."

"I wonder what *that* was all about," exclaimed George. "It reminded me of a scene from a detective show or something." She gazed down the street where the cars had disappeared.

"Hmm," said Emily thoughtfully. "We may have just seen an example of some of the mob activity Lieutenant Chin mentioned."

"Did you get a look at either of the drivers?" Nancy asked her.

"No. Unfortunately, I was still thinking about our bald guy. If only I'd had my camera. Taking pictures is second nature to me. I guarantee we would have had the whole thing captured on film."

Nancy nodded. "I didn't notice much, either," she said. "What about you, Hannah?"

"Nothing. Maybe something will come to me after I've had a chance to think."

"Right," Emily agreed. "Okay. Back to my place. Only forget the cab. We'll walk."

A half-hour later, Nancy, George, and Hannah were following Emily through the door of her cozy apartment.

"Oh, I love it!" cried George, looking around at the art deco lamps that cast a warm glow on the overstuffed furniture in the living room.

Emily grinned. "Thanks," she replied. "Meet Tripod." She lifted the cover off a large bird cage. "Say hello, Tripod."

"Hello. Hello."

The others laughed as the blue-fronted Amazon parrot greeted them in his high voice.

"Any time someone is in the room, Tripod starts talking," Emily told them. "He never shuts up. But I love him. He's a great companion."

"What's for dessert?" the bird asked.

"Yes," said Hannah, laughing. "What *is* for dessert? You promised us some of your cooking. Emily is one of the best chefs around, girls. Years ago, we used to have cooking contests, trying to outdo each other."

"Well, I admit I bake a pretty tasty cake," Emily said. "But I could never come close to Hannah's pot roast. Do you still make a mean pot roast, Hannah?"

"Does she ever!" Nancy volunteered, and Hannah blushed.

While Emily made coffee and cut slices of something she called chocolate swirl cake, the girls admired the apartment.

"Feel free to browse around," said Emily. "Take a look at the darkroom. It's my pride and joy."

Nancy and George poked their noses into Emily's studio. Nancy, who knew something about photography, admired the enlarger. George was impressed by how neatly organized Emily kept her supplies.

"I develop all my own film," Emily called from the kitchen. "I don't trust anyone else to do it for

22

me. Sometimes I get lost in there. I get started on a project, and when I come out, half the day has gone by."

Nancy and George returned to the kitchen, where Emily handed them their dessert. "But I love my work," she went on. "I wouldn't have it any other way."

George took a bite of the cake. "Wow, this is great!" she exclaimed.

"Definitely," agreed Nancy. While she ate, she studied the photos that covered Emily's walls. "Which picture won the photojournalism award?" Emily had once been the winner of the most prestigious award given to a photographer.

"The one to the left of Tripod's cage is the winner," Emily replied, handing Hannah a cup of coffee.

Nancy got up to take a closer look. "Who's that man?"

"His name is Harold Kesack."

Nancy stared into a shifty-looking face.

"He was a well-known crime leader," Emily explained. "He died in a private plane crash just before he was supposed to face a grand jury investigation. It was an odd coincidence. That happened about five years ago."

Nancy peered closely at the photo. "Look at the Buddha he's wearing around his neck. I've never seen anything like it. It's beautiful."

"That was Kesack's trademark. It was carved out of ivory. It intrigued me, too. I asked him about it when I interviewed him. Kesack said he wore it all the time. The rumor was that it had been a gift from some big member of the Chinese mob. Of course, I didn't ask him to verify *that.*"

Nancy continued to study the photo. "And that huge scar on his chin. How awful. It's almost evil-looking."

"That," Emily said, "was supposedly the result of a gang fight in prison. Kesack ended up in the middle of the pack. I didn't verify that bit of information, either."

Hannah shuddered. "Emily, honest to goodness, the people you know!"

But Nancy laughed. "She didn't say he was a friend, Hannah."

"Well, I should hope not."

Emily was philosophical. "You meet all sorts in my profession. I guess that's why I enjoy it so much. I can't see myself stuck behind some desk eight hours a day. Each experience is new, each story is different."

"What's for dessert?" Tripod squawked again.

"Oh, all right, you silly bird." Emily fed Tripod a bit of cake. The parrot held it daintily in one foot, tasted it, then gobbled it down.

"What a pig!" George exclaimed.

"His favorite food is spaghetti," Emily said, and everyone laughed.

When they stopped, silence fell over the room. Even Tripod quieted down and sat contemplating the guests.

"Hannah, even if we had this recipe, I bet we couldn't make a cake this good." Nancy smiled at Emily.

"We'll just have to invite Emily to River Heights for a pot roast dinner," said Hannah.

"I'd like that," Emily replied sincerely. "And I'll bring dessert."

Nancy was about to get up to examine Emily's photos again when the phone rang. Emily excused herself and went into the kitchen.

From the living room, Nancy could see Emily talking on the phone. She watched as her expression turned from friendly anticipation to concern. Then Nancy saw Emily's face turn white. The photographer dropped the receiver to the floor.

Nancy ran to her side. "Emily! What is it?"

Emily didn't answer.

Nancy picked up the receiver. "Hello? Hello?" she said. The line clicked dead. Nancy turned her attention back to Emily, whose color was returning. "Emily, what's wrong? What happened? Who was that?"

By now, George and Hannah had joined them in the kitchen. Concern showed on their faces.

"I don't know," Emily replied slowly. "But whoever it was told me in no uncertain terms to drop the 'Children of Change' story. Or else!"

4

The Man in the Street

Nancy realized she was still holding the phone receiver. The dial tone droned into the silence of the kitchen. She replaced the receiver and motioned everyone back into the warm light of the living room.

"Well, all I can say is, I'm not about to drop the 'Children of Change' story," Emily declared immediately. "I don't care who tells me to!" She smiled ruefully at Hannah. "Life is really not this exciting all the time around here, although you probably don't believe that after today."

"Do you have any idea who was on the phone?" Nancy asked quietly.

"No. I don't have a very good memory for voices, but I'm sure I would have recognized this one if I'd heard it before," Emily answered.

"Why would you recognize the voice again? Was it male or female? Was there an accent?"

"It was just a man's voice, Nancy, but it was sort of low and harsh. . . . Maybe he was trying to disguise it."

Hannah stood up to get more coffee. She looked carefully at her old friend. "Are you sure you're okay, Emily? I need another cup of coffee. Do you want one, too?"

"Oh, I'm fine, Hannah. It's just not every day I receive threatening phone calls."

"Emily." Nancy leaned forward. "Do you have any enemies?"

Emily laughed. "There are probably plenty of people who'd like to see me out of their way, but I don't think I have any real enemies. I guess Peter Stine would be the most glad to see me out of action, though."

Hannah brought in fresh cups of coffee for herself and Emily and settled on the couch again to listen.

"Tell me about Stine, Emily," Nancy said.

"There's not that much to tell, really," she replied, "except that for years now, there's been a rivalry between us—a competition. Stine works for a newspaper on the other side of San Francisco Bay, in Marin County. But there's nothing threatening about him. We're just two professionals who've been assigned to the same stories for years.

"I always beat him to the punch on the top

stories, one way or another," she went on. "Which bothers him, naturally."

Emily, relaxing a bit, began to chuckle. Tripod, echoing the chuckle, made everyone jump. Then they laughed when he squawked and fluffed his feathers, as if embarrassed to have disturbed them.

Emily began to tell about the time she had gotten a tip from one of her underground contacts regarding a hot story that was breaking and was at the scene, taking pictures, a good half-hour before Stine or anyone else showed up.

As she talked, Nancy glanced around the apartment. She wondered what it was that would put Emily in jeopardy. Why would anyone threaten her, especially about "Children of Change," a story in which no crime was being exposed and no accusations were being made? The apartment was cozy and homelike; the darkroom was clean and efficient. And all the criminals represented here, thought Nancy, studying the photos on the walls, are either behind bars or, like Harold Kesack, dead.

Nancy stood near the window and looked out onto the street below, only half-listening to Emily's stories. Out of the corner of her eye, she noticed someone standing by the curb. She started to turn back to the others, but something made her look again at the figure below.

It was a man, thin and wiry, with a light jacket

28

pulled tightly around him. He wasn't very tall. Then Nancy realized why he had attracted her attention. He was watching the house, looking up at the windows of Emily's apartment from time to time, while pretending to be waiting for a cab or a bus. Wasn't he? Nancy was sure of it after she saw a bus draw up to the curb, then move on, leaving the man still standing on the street.

Nancy moved away from the window and walked over to the easy chair George was lounging in. She gave George a quick nudge and smiled at Hannah and Emily. "Here we are in San Francisco, and you and Emily haven't had a minute to yourselves, Hannah," she said. "George and I need to go walk off some of the calories from that cake, don't we, George? We'll leave you here so you can do some catching up."

George didn't need a second nudge to tell her that Nancy had a reason for wanting to go for a walk. Her years of friendship with Nancy had taught her to trust Nancy's instincts and to be ready for whatever adventures lay ahead. She stood up and stretched.

"Yeah. I'd like to see this neighborhood. It sure doesn't look like River Heights."

"In my opinion, both of you girls could use the extra calories." Hannah sniffed, studying Nancy and George. "You're both too thin. But go ahead and take a walk."

Emily cautioned the girls to stay on well-lit

streets, assuring Hannah that they'd be all right as long as they didn't go into any dark alleys or wander into the nearby industrial district.

"Don't worry about us. We'll be careful." Nancy waved Hannah and Emily back to their coffee and dessert as she and George moved toward the door, just out of sight of the window.

They shut the door behind them and stood in the stairwell. George whispered, "What's up, Nan? You have that look on your face that you always get when there's a mystery about to happen."

"You're right. Thanks for coming with me. Listen—someone's watching Emily's apartment."

"Are you sure?"

Nancy told George what she'd seen. She explained that she hoped they could get a good look at the man and that she didn't want any noises to alert him that he'd been noticed. They crept down the steps silently. Maybe if they just walked out the door onto the porch, he would think they were from the first-floor apartment and wouldn't pay attention to them.

At the bottom of the stairs, George cautiously pulled back the curtain on the front door—just enough to look out. The man was still there, a silhouette in the streetlight. He was staring intently at the windows of Emily's upstairs apartment.

Nancy opened the door, and she and George

casually stepped outside, trying to talk and laugh as if they were just going out to get an ice cream from down the street. The man looked startled for a moment, then turned as if to resume his watch. But as Nancy and George set off in his direction, he seemed to change his mind and started walking rapidly down the street away from them.

The girls exchanged glances and followed him. "Ned really wished he could have come with us," Nancy said to George in a loud voice, hoping the man wouldn't think they were following him. Earlier in the day, Nancy had been thinking about her boyfriend, Ned Nickerson, who was busy with exams at Emerson College and wouldn't be free until after Nancy returned from California. "Ned would have liked Chinatown," Nancy went on, acting as if nothing were wrong.

But it didn't do much good. The man looked back once or twice but kept increasing his pace until, after a block or two, he was nearly running. Nancy and George finally dropped all efforts to act like they were out for a casual stroll, and they hurried after him.

"Maybe there's a car waiting for him, or he'll go into a house or an office or something," George suggested.

But he did none of those things. In the middle of a block that was only partially lit by the tall, old-fashioned street lamps, the man ducked down an alley. He was immediately swallowed up

31

by the darkness of the closed-in alley. Remembering Emily's warning, Nancy stared for a moment into the blackness, then sighed and motioned to George that they should give up.

"We can't keep chasing him, especially when we can't even see him!"

The girls walked swiftly back to Emily's, intent on the mystery at hand. By the time they got back, they were able to put on the appearance of two friends who had just had a nice evening walk. Hannah and Emily were smiling and relaxed as well.

The girls picked up the empty dessert dishes and coffee cups and cleared away the crumbs, laughing when Tripod scolded them and offered his chatty parrot advice. Hannah yawned, looked at her watch, and gave a start. "Good heavens, girls, do you know it's nearly midnight?"

"No, it's not, Hannah." Nancy smiled. "That's River Heights time. It's two hours earlier here in San Francisco. You'd better reset your watch."

"Well, my body is still on River Heights time," protested George.

"All three of you look like you need a good night's sleep," said Emily. She dialed a number she apparently knew well and asked for a cab to come to her address. After another moment or two of conversation, she shepherded her guests toward the door.

They paused long enough to make plans for the next day. Emily suggested that if the weather was

32

clear, it would be a good day for a sightseeing tour she had read about, and the others agreed. They arranged a time and a place to meet, and then Nancy, George, and Hannah called good night to Emily and walked tiredly down the steps.

Nancy looked for the thin, wiry man as they stepped onto the porch, but he was nowhere to be seen. The street was empty and silent. Hannah yawned again and commented that she hoped the hotel bed was a good one. At that moment, a cab rounded the corner a block or two down the street and headed their way. As it pulled up in front of the house, Nancy stepped back to let Hannah and George in first. Hannah was just bending down to get into the backseat, when a woman's scream, loud and piercing, echoed in the night.

"That was Emily!" exclaimed Hannah.

5

Interrupted Goodbyes

Without a word to the confused cab driver, Nancy rushed back to Emily's apartment with George and Hannah right behind her. Her heart thudded in her chest as she took the stairs two at a time. She pounded on the door. "Emily!" she yelled. "Emily! Are you all right?"

Emily opened the door. She stood before Nancy, brandishing a broom. "Yes," she replied disgustedly. "I'm all right. But he got away."

"Who? Who got away?" demanded Hannah and George.

"The man who was trying to get in through my skylight." Emily pointed to the ceiling. The skylight above, which was large enough for a man to crawl through, was open. Nancy looked up at the moon shining through it. She asked Emily for

34

a stepstool, then reached up and closed the skylight.

Climbing down, she asked, "Did you see what he looked like?"

"Like most cat burglars, I suppose," Emily answered. She sounded annoyed. "He was dressed in black. Black pants, shirt, gloves. Black ski hat. That's all I saw."

"What about his features? How old was he?" Nancy asked.

"I couldn't say. I really didn't see."

"Emily," Hannah said, exasperated, "I don't like this at all."

"No cat burglar is going to mess with Emily Foxworth! I almost had him. I whomped him a good one on the leg. He won't come prowling around here again!" Emily flailed at the air with her broom, demonstrating how she had attacked the intruder.

"Well, I think it might be a good idea if we spent the night. Just to be on hand if he comes back to try again." Nancy looked at Hannah and George, who nodded in agreement.

"Shouldn't we call the police?" Hannah asked.

"Probably," Nancy answered. "But I doubt if they'll find him. He's long gone by now."

Hannah was not convinced. "Still, an alert might save someone else in the neighborhood."

"I suppose you're right, Hannah." Emily went to the phone to report the attempted break-in. When she returned, she told the others that the police had radioed a patrol car to be on the lookout for the intruder. "I don't like to inconvenience you," Emily said, "but I'm glad you're staying. Fortunately, I have plenty of beds. Nancy and George can have the couch—it pulls out. And there's a daybed in my room. I'll sleep on that, Hannah. You can have my bed."

Hannah sat down on the couch and crossed her arms over her chest. "It's not an inconvenience, Emily. Don't be silly. Tomorrow, we can just stop off at our hotel for a change of clothing. And *I'll* take the daybed," she said firmly.

Nancy and George exchanged suppressed smiles.

"All right," Emily said. "Now, off the couch. I don't know about you three, but I'm beat." She pulled out the couch. "There are sheets and blankets in the linen closet—"

"I'll get them," George interrupted, moving toward the closet Emily had indicated.

"And I'll make up the daybed," Hannah said, following George.

"Okay. Meanwhile, I'll try to round up something for each of you to sleep in."

Nancy and George had the couch half made up when a knock sounded at the door. "We'll get it," Nancy called.

With George standing beside her, Nancy fastened the chain on the door before opening it. Two uniformed police officers stood outside. She unlatched the chain and let them in.

The officers questioned Emily and assured her that they would be patrolling the neighborhood all night long.

"We'll keep watch," the female officer said. "You shouldn't have any more trouble."

Not long after the officers left, Nancy and the others settled in for the night. Nancy could hear Emily and Hannah whispering faintly to each other in the other room.

"George?" she murmured. "George?"

George's even breathing was the only response Nancy heard. Nancy was tired, too, but even so, she tried to piece together the day's events: first there was the theft of the camera, then the bald man who had followed them through Chinatown, then the cars that had almost run Hannah down, the threatening phone call to Emily, the man watching the apartment, and finally the attempted break-in. Were these incidents related? Were they coincidence? Nancy wasn't sure, but she decided to begin a further investigation. In the morning, while the others went off sightseeing, she would go in search of Peter Stine. The mystery, if it was a mystery, intrigued her. It was a long time before she slept.

As they walked to the hotel early the next morning, Nancy told Emily what she had decided to do. Emily agreed that a talk with Peter Stine might be helpful. "But perhaps I should go with you," she added.

37

"No," Nancy said. "I want to confront him alone. You enjoy your day of sightseeing with Hannah and George. After all, you're on vacation, too."

Emily laughed. "Some vacation so far. For all of us. But I can help. You'll need transportation, and I have a friend with a very generous nature *and* a car. I'll call him from your hotel."

Following Emily's directions, Nancy drove to Marin County to see the journalist who was Emily's rival. The morning was crisp and clear. Puffy white clouds hung in the sky. Nancy hummed to herself as she drove past Fisherman's Wharf and Ghirardelli Square. As she approached the Golden Gate Bridge, she saw the handsome Spanish-style buildings of the Presidio, the famous army base tucked against the lush green hills overlooking the bay. The Golden Gate itself was breathtaking, its huge steel girders reaching to the sky. Arriving on the other side of the bridge, Nancy took note of the rugged terrain on her left, the cliffs hugging the bay, and, farther away, the California farmland. On her right was the little city of Sausalito, famous for its colony of houseboats.

Twenty minutes later, Nancy entered the office of the Marin County newspaper where Peter Stine worked. Long rows of desks, each equipped with a computer terminal, filled the large open room. Nancy stared at the employees. Some were rereading text and editing; others were keyboarding new material into their consoles.

"May I help you?" The attractive receptionist smiled at Nancy.

"Yes," she replied. "I'm here to see Peter Stine."

"Right this way." Nancy followed the woman to a private office. "Mr. Stine, a young woman is here to see you."

"Yes?" The man looked up from his desk. Even though he was sitting down, Nancy could tell that Peter Stine was tall and lanky. He had bushy eyebrows, thinning hair, and a fierce expression. Nancy judged him to be about fifty. He gave the impression of being annoyed by the intrusion.

"Peter Stine? My name's Nancy Drew." Nancy extended her hand, but he ignored it.

"What do you want?" he grumbled.

Nancy decided on the direct approach. "I'm a detective, and I need to ask you a few questions. Do you know who might be responsible for a threatening phone call to Emily Foxworth?"

Stine snorted rudely. "Emily Foxworth sticks her nose in where it doesn't belong," he replied. "Any threats she's received are no doubt due."

Was that another threat? Nancy took an immediate dislike to the gruff reporter, although she tried not to show it.

"If that's all you came here for—to ask questions about Foxworth—I'm going to have to ask you to leave," said Stine. "I have work to do."

"Peter? You're wanted in Taylor's office. Pronto." A young reporter handed a message to Stine, smiled at Nancy, and disappeared.

"Excuse me, miss . . . What was your name?"

"Drew. Nancy Drew."

Stine pushed passed her. "I really don't have any time right now."

As soon as Nancy was certain the journalist was well away from his office, she took the opportunity to peek at the paperwork on his desk. Several notes pertaining to mob activity and gang bosses in the city caught her eye. She was trying to commit the information to memory when she heard Stine returning.

He stepped back into his office. "You still here?" He raised one bushy eyebrow.

Nancy smiled innocently. "I dropped my purse. You know what a mess that can be. Everything scattered."

Stine sat back down at his desk. "You're interrupting my work," he said pointedly.

Nancy felt her face flush with anger, but she tried to stay calm. "Goodbye, Mr. Stine," she said icily, and she left the office.

The visit to Stine's office had revealed nothing, except that Emily's rival was apparently working on a story about the increase of mobster activity in San Francisco. But that had no connection to Emily. When Lieutenant Chin had mentioned the increased mob activity to Emily, she'd told him she was "off duty." Nancy, trying to put the pieces together, felt frustrated. She just didn't have enough information yet. And she felt angry that the reporter had been so rude. Was he hiding something? Nancy thought he was a nasty enough person to have made the phone call to Emily. And he hadn't denied making it. But that certainly wasn't evidence or proof. All the way back across the Golden Gate Bridge and into San Francisco, she reviewed the mysterious events of her vacation.

After returning the borrowed car to Emily's friend, Nancy took a cable car to Fisherman's Wharf. As she walked the three blocks to the wharf, she glanced at her watch. She began to walk faster. She'd agreed to meet George, Hannah, and Emily at twelve-thirty, and she didn't want to be late. Then she saw George waving to her.

"Hurry up, Nancy!" George called. "I'm starving."

Nancy laughed. "You sound just like Bess," she said, joining the others.

They ate lunch in a restaurant that looked out over the bay.

"I know I said I was starving, but this is the biggest crab salad I've ever seen!" George exclaimed. "Where am I supposed to put it all?"

"In any space you haven't already filled up with sourdough bread," Nancy replied.

"I'm going to buy a carload of the stuff and ship

it home," George announced. "Bess will kill me—but she'll love it."

"Everyone loves it," Emily said. "It's famous. Best in the west."

"Wait till she tastes the chocolate," Hannah said.

"What chocolate?" Nancy asked.

Hannah described their visit to Ghirardelli Square that morning. "The chocolate from there is world famous, and I bought several packages to take home to River Heights," she said with a smile.

"Another ride on the cable cars?" Emily suggested as they left the restaurant.

"I'd like that," George said. "But I wouldn't mind walking around some more first."

They decided on a stroll to the far end of the wharf, where Emily could take some photos of the boats that were loading and unloading.

Hannah was intrigued by the bay, the smell of the ocean, the street vendors hawking their wares. Emily shot one photo after another. By this time, everyone was comfortable with the familiar click of Emily's camera.

Nancy found herself looking at things from a new perspective—through the eyes of a photographer, grasping details even her own trained eyes might have missed. She and Emily took off ahead of George and Hannah, who walked at a more leisurely pace behind them.

Suddenly, as Nancy and Emily were passing one of the larger boats moored at the dock, they heard George cry, "Nancy! Emily! Run!"

Nancy looked up—just in time to see a netful of packing crates falling toward them with terrifying speed!

6

Break-in

Nancy leaped aside, pulling Emily with her. They fell onto a pile of filled canvas bags just as the net and its contents smashed to the wharf. The crates landed inches from them and shattered with a sickening crash. Nancy jumped to her feet instantly and helped Emily up from the jumble of sacks.

"It's a good thing some ship unloaded its laundry here as a mattress for us!" Nancy commented ruefully as she and Emily rubbed bruised joints. Then they checked Emily's camera and light meter to be sure they hadn't been damaged in the fall.

They turned to see George and Hannah, their faces anxious, trying to get around the wreckage, maneuvering between the netting and the broken crates.

"George, thank you for warning us," Emily exclaimed. "If you hadn't, Nancy and I would have been pressed duck!" Emily's voice was shaky, but her sense of humor was still with her.

A sheepish-looking dockworker walked over to where Nancy and her friends were standing and studied the broken cargo. "Somebody slipped up," he muttered.

"I should say so!" Hannah retorted angrily.

"Yeah, but it was an accident," another dockworker said. He stood off to one side with a third man. Then the three of them moved slowly toward the mess, as if intending to clean it up—eventually.

Nancy glanced at George and nodded in the direction of the workers. "Didn't you say you and Hannah wanted to find out how these wharves are used, George?" she asked.

As Nancy had hoped, George took the hint, and she and then Hannah began asking the men about the docks, the ships, and the cargo. George made sure they moved just far enough away so that Nancy and Emily could look over the wreckage.

Emily snapped photos, clicking away at whatever Nancy indicated might be important. Nancy held up the ropes that had bound the sturdy netting together. "There's no sign that the ropes were cut or tampered with," she pointed out. "They're still strong and intact." And the netting, although tangled from the fall, was still whole. The shattered crates revealed nothing.

Nancy glanced around the wharf, in search of clues. Then she looked upward at the cable dangling high above her head. The coupling clamp was *open*. The massive clamp, Nancy knew, was controlled by levers on the crane that the cable was attached to. Nancy stared at it. "Emily," she whispered, "how can we tell if the cargo was deliberately released by the crane operator?"

"I don't know," Emily replied. "Maybe the clamp just slipped."

Nancy was going to ask Emily to get a shot of the crane—until she noticed that the crane operator was still seated at the controls! He looked as if he hadn't even noticed the accident, but that would have been almost impossible. Maybe, Nancy thought, he deliberately didn't notice it. His pale face was long and hard. And his eyes were cold, and so dark they appeared black. With a shiver, Nancy realized that she wouldn't need one of Emily's photographs to remember that face.

Suddenly, Nancy laughed and moved toward her friends. "Let's leave this place and go downtown for some fun," she suggested, hoping to convince the man who was watching them from the crane that they weren't too concerned about the accident after all. Nancy, George, Hannah, and Emily accepted the dockworkers' apologies and assured them that they understood that accidents happen. They walked back toward the street.

"Whew. I don't know what happened there, but I could use a moment to catch my breath," Emily said, heaving a sigh.

"Me, too." Nancy glanced back at the docks. The three men were shoving the net and its contents aside in order to make room for other containers that needed to be unloaded. The crane operator still sat inside the cab.

"Why don't we sit down for a while?" suggested Emily, and Nancy felt relieved when Hannah spotted some benches. Her mind was racing.

"I wonder if that accident just now had anything to do with the telephone call Emily received last night," Nancy whispered to George. George shook her head and shrugged. Nancy found it hard to believe that Emily Foxworth might have enemies. She still wasn't sure about Peter Stine, but she didn't think he could have known they would be on the wharf that afternoon. The situation was baffling.

Everyone was quiet as they made their way back to Emily's apartment through San Francisco's heavy late-afternoon traffic. When they reached it, Tripod, as usual, began to chatter. But the scene that greeted them was not the one they had left that morning. The apartment was a mess.

"I don't believe it!" Emily cried, stepping into the living room and staring, horrified, at the chaos. Nancy and George went into action immediately. They checked the rest of the apartment to be sure that no intruder was still around.

In each room, furniture and possessions were strewn about. Drawers had been opened and their contents dumped to the floor. But nothing seemed to have been damaged or destroyed, which indicated to Nancy that the burglar or burglars had been looking for something specific.

"Emily, you should call the police," Hannah said firmly, and Emily picked up the phone and called Lieutenant Chin.

When she hung up, Nancy asked Emily if she could tell if anything had been stolen. She was beginning to wonder if this incident were connected to the "accident" on the docks, and whether it was all some kind of plot to frighten Emily.

"My cameras!" Emily exclaimed, and she ran to her darkroom to check her equipment. Nancy urged Emily not to touch anything until the police arrived, but they did notice that all of the cameras had been opened, revealing the empty film chambers, and that the film magazines had been removed and scattered. This was no ordinary robbery, Nancy realized. Hundreds of dollars' worth of equipment lay strewn on the counters and in the open drawers. Expensive light meters, electronic flash and strobe units, motor drives, and several lenses, all of which could easily have been taken and resold by a thief, had been left behind.

"All my cameras are still here," Emily announced. Relieved, she began to inspect the rest of the apartment. As far as she could tell, nothing was missing.

"Except for my photos . . ." Emily began. She stared at the walls in the living room, and as Nancy and the others joined her, they realized that a few pictures were missing from her informal gallery near the sofa. Nancy noticed that the intriguing shot of Harold Kesack was among those that had been taken. She returned to the hallway and the bedrooms and saw other gaps where clusters of photos had hung.

Before the police arrived and began to ask their questions, Nancy made some mental notes. "The negative files are a mess," she observed as she returned to the darkroom. Why had someone apparently gone after selected photos and then tried to get the negatives, too?

Returning to the living room, Nancy stopped when she noticed a slip of paper blow across the floor. She looked up, wondering where the breeze was coming from, and saw the open skylight. This time, an intruder had succeeded in entering through the window in the roof.

Nancy continued her inspection, looking for footprints or any other evidence that might be helpful. She found only a small folded piece of paper in one corner of the room. She opened it to find the numbers "37-4-11-12" scrawled in dark ink. She puzzled over them for a moment, then folded the paper and stuck it in the pocket of her jeans, just as footsteps could be heard coming up the stairs outside Emily's apartment.

Emily answered the knock and let the police in—a uniformed officer from the neighborhood and Lieutenant Chin.

"Emily, you're calling me all the time now," the lieutenant teased her. "Don't you think you're taking advantage of our friendship?" He greeted the others and introduced everyone to Officer Johnson.

Both men examined the apartment. Then they questioned Emily and her guests about the break-in and robbery. Nancy mentioned that none of Emily's photographic equipment had been stolen.

"The only things missing are some photos off the walls," Emily said, clearly puzzled.

"Are you sure you aren't making enemies by investigating some hot news story?" asked the lieutenant.

"I'm sure, Don. You've seen my pictures. And now I'm working on the urban children story. Who would be angry with me because I'm photographing little kids?"

"You're right. It doesn't make sense. This is a strange one. I'll stay in touch and see if I can't move the investigation along for you. Keep me filled in on anything else you think might be related, all right?"

"You ought to know about an incident that happened down at the docks today, Lieutenant Chin." Nancy spoke up. She described the accident to the police officer. Hannah and George told the officers what they had seen.

"Also, Hannah was nearly hit by a couple of speeding cars yesterday," Nancy said. "I thought at the time that they were just reckless drivers, but with everything else that's been happening, I'm not so sure now." Nancy gave the lieutenant a description of the cars and told him where the incident had occurred.

Chin looked startled, then concerned. "I'm not happy to hear this," he said. "One of those cars is a perfect match for one we spotted yesterday, one we believe belongs to a syndicate man—one of their leaders."

"Donald, there are always syndicate men around here. Why are you so worried?" Emily wanted to know.

"Because right now there are a few more than normal. Our men at the airport and around the waterfront report seeing a lot of characters who haven't been seen or heard from in years. There are some big names in from Chicago. Seattle, too." The lieutenant went on to describe sightings of some known syndicate strong-arms and hit men.

"Why are they all gathering in San Francisco right now?" Nancy asked.

"We're not sure yet. That's what worries us. We're quite certain that something big is about to happen. It takes a major operation for these types to risk being seen together where we're so familiar with their faces. But we're not even sure where to look or, for that matter, what to look for or when to look for it."

The officers completed their inspection of Emily's apartment and asked her to sign their report. Then they gathered up their equipment and got ready to leave.

Lieutenant Chin hesitated at the door. He looked at Emily soberly. "I don't know what's happening here, but I want you to watch out for yourself," he told her. "Let me know if you see or hear anything unusual, or even if you just think something might be wrong. Is that clear?"

Emily agreed, insisting that she couldn't think of a reason why anyone would try to do more than scare her.

Nancy watched the departing officers. She thought they seemed worried. She looked at Emily and shivered. Whatever was wrong, Nancy was suddenly certain that Emily Foxworth was somehow in the middle of it, and that the photographer's life was in real danger.

7

The Dark Room

"Emily," Nancy said, "I'm not sure what exactly is going on here, although it must have something to do with your photographs. If you don't mind, I'd like to see your exhibit at the gallery. Maybe a clue, a missing link, will be found there. Why don't we help you clean up this mess, and then I'll go to the gallery?"

"Why don't we all go?" Hannah suggested. "We haven't been there yet, and I'd love to see Emily's other work."

"Good idea." Emily picked up a broken candy dish and dropped it in a wastebasket. "I'd like to make sure everything is in order there, anyway."

Working together, the four replaced drawers and restocked cupboards and shelves with

Emily's possessions. Hannah put Emily's books back in the cases, George hung up clothes, and Emily and Nancy straightened up the darkroom. They closed the camera backs and returned the negatives to the file case.

When everything was cleaned up, Emily telephoned for a taxi. Fifteen minutes later, Nancy and her friends were entering the gallery, housed in a large brick building. The gallery was well lit and decorated in gray and maroon. Nancy stepped onto lush carpeting, aware of the quiet. Bronzes sat on pedestals in the middle of the room. Several oils by one artist and some watercolors by another hung on freshly painted walls.

Nancy watched as George stood before an abstract painting, fascinated by the vibrancy of its colors and its suggestive forms.

"Where are your photographs?" Hannah whispered to Emily.

"Next room," Emily replied, escorting the group through a doorway.

"Emily," Nancy said immediately, "your photos are wonderful!"

But Emily stared at the walls, a look of annoyance crossing her face.

"What's wrong?" Hannah asked her.

"Huh? Oh, it's just that some of my work isn't up yet. Faith promised everything would be set up and ready. I guess I'd better go find her. Not only do I have to *take* the pictures, I have to *hang* them as well."

54

"Want some help?" George offered.

"Thanks. I can handle it. The rest are probably right where I left them, in my portfolio in the storeroom. I'll go check."

Hannah and George decided to browse through the rest of the gallery, while Nancy took a close look at each of Emily's photos, searching for . . . she wasn't sure what.

She was standing in front of one of them when a voice said, "They're lovely, aren't they?"

Nancy turned around to face a heavyset woman who appeared to be in her late forties. She wore a loud pants suit, and her hair was dyed a bright, brassy blond. The woman extended her hand. "I'm Faith Arnold. I own the gallery. And the photos you're admiring are the work of Emily—"

"I'm a friend of Emily's," Nancy interrupted her.

"Oh."

Nancy thought she detected a change in the woman's tone of voice. "Emily's gone to check the storeroom for the rest of her photos," she added. "She says some of them aren't on display." She eyed the woman steadily. Faith Arnold looked distinctly uncomfortable. Nancy was about to ask her a few questions when she realized that Emily had been gone much longer than necessary.

At that moment, a movement outside the window of the gallery caused Nancy to forget about

Faith Arnold. Nancy suddenly saw the same thin, wiry man she and George had followed outside Emily's apartment. "George!" she yelled, running to the door.

Nancy was out the door in seconds, with George in hot pursuit. They stopped at the corner, looking up and down the street.

"What is it?" George asked, trying to catch her breath. "You took off so fast—"

"I saw him."

"Who?"

"The same guy we chased before. Outside Emily's. But it looks like we lost him again."

"I wonder what he wants. Why is he watching us?"

"I don't know. If we could talk to him, some of this mystery would be cleared up."

The girls quickly returned to the art gallery. Nancy found Hannah and asked her if she'd seen Emily.

Hannah shook her head. "Not since she disappeared into the storeroom."

Uh-oh, thought Nancy, but she just said lightly, "Let's go see what's taking her so long."

Faith Arnold was busy showing a customer some artwork, so Nancy, George, and Hannah decided to find their own way to the back of the building. They reached a door marked "Storage," which Nancy opened, only to be met by blackness.

"Turn on the lights," said George.

As Nancy fumbled for the light switch, she heard a scuffle at the far end of the room.

"Help!" came Emily's frantic call. Nancy rushed into the room, forgetting to look for the lights. As their eyes adjusted to the darkness, she, George, and Hannah saw the figures of two men pulling Emily out the back door and into an alley.

Nancy threw herself at one of the assailants and subdued him with a well-placed karate kick. Emily fought hard, biting and scratching the man who held her firmly in his grip. George joined the struggle then, but she was shoved roughly against a wall, while Nancy was pushed to the floor by the recovered kidnapper.

Hannah stood silently in stunned disbelief as the two men raced out the door with their struggling victim. As soon as they had gone, she ran to George and Nancy. "Are you all right?" she cried.

The girls stood up shakily and found that they were bruised but otherwise unhurt.

Nancy wasted no time in running outside and down the alley after the kidnappers. She reached the street just in time to see the men shove Emily through the door of a waiting limousine. The driver gunned the engine, and the limousine jerked forward, hitting a trash can and sending garbage flying everywhere. Nancy, out of breath, quit running when she realized that the car's license plates had been covered with mud and she had no way of identifying the vehicle. Sadly, she returned to George and Hannah. She had to tell them that Emily Foxworth was gone.

8

Trailing the Tail

Rubbing her bruised arm, which was beginning to throb, Nancy ducked through the back door into the gloomy storeroom. George finally found the switchplate and turned the lights on.

"Let's get a good look around here before anyone comes in and destroys possible evidence," Nancy suggested. "And, Hannah, why don't you find a phone and get hold of Lieutenant Chin?"

Hannah merely nodded, obviously frightened, and left the storeroom quickly.

George and Nancy scoured the warehouselike room for clues. Near the door, Nancy found Emily's camera. It was lying open on the floor. When she looked at it closely, but without touching it, she discovered that it had been deliberately broken. The lens had been smashed hard against the concrete floor. The camera back had been torn open, its hinges bent. And the film spools had been ripped from their sockets. The film itself was missing, except for a shred that clung to the sprockets near the shutter.

"Nancy, do you think this might be important?" Nancy looked up from the camera. George was pointing to a handle which was lying on a stack of packing boxes. Like the camera, it had been broken, probably yanked off something. Also like the camera, the damage appeared to have been done quickly and violently. Part of the case that the handle was once fastened to was still hanging from a twisted hinge.

"Maybe it's one of the handles from Emily's portfolio case," George murmured.

"That's a good possibility," replied Nancy, taking a closer look at the handle. "Maybe the case is still around here somewhere." She and George searched the room for the portfolio, but Nancy had a feeling they weren't going to find it.

Faith Arnold appeared in the doorway then. She cleared her throat. "I, uh . . ." She hesitated.

Nancy turned toward her.

"The case . . . it's . . . well, I think . . . if it was the portfolio I left here earlier. . . ." Faith Arnold ran a hand nervously through her hair, brushing her bangs back from her face. "There were several photos of Emily's in it. They were for the exhibit."

"Emily's been kidnapped," Nancy told her flatly. "The police are on the way."

Faith Arnold straightened up. "Oh, no," she said softly. "I don't believe it . . . I suppose I ought to go wait for them."

Lieutenant Chin showed up a few moments later, dressed in street clothes. Nancy, George, and Hannah met him at the front of the gallery. This time, he didn't smile when he greeted them. Nancy introduced him to Faith Arnold, and then he grimly began questioning the four about the events surrounding Emily's kidnapping.

Just as Nancy and Faith Arnold were about to lead the lieutenant back to the storeroom, Peter Stine marched into the gallery. He walked directly over to the group. "I just happened to be in the neighborhood and heard about the ruckus," he said. He grinned at Nancy.

"I don't see what you're smiling about," she replied sharply.

"What are you doing here?" Chin asked him. "Looking for a story, I suppose?" Without waiting for a reply, the lieutenant turned back to the women, asking them how the kidnappers had taken Emily.

"The lights were out," Nancy explained. "But those guys seemed to know their way around." She described the struggle.

"I'll put out an all-points bulletin on the limo,

Nancy. I wish you could give me a clearer description of the men. Is there anything else I should know about?" Lieutenant Chin scribbled hastily in his small notebook. Nancy glanced at George and Hannah and shook her head.

"Not that I can think of, Lieutenant." She didn't mention the missing photos or the man who'd followed them. Stine, asking questions, drew Lieutenant Chin away from Nancy. She quickly whispered to Hannah and George, "I don't know whom to trust anymore. I think we've been watched ever since we arrived in San Francisco. But by whom? The police? Stine? The mob?"

George nodded in agreement. "I know what you mean," she said.

Lieutenant Chin turned abruptly away from Peter Stine. "I'll look at the storeroom now," he said to Nancy. "The rest of you"—he glared at Stine—"can wait here. We won't be long."

Lieutenant Chin glanced around the storeroom. He noted the smashed camera on the floor and the handle lying on the packing case. "Probably won't be any fingerprints," he said, "but I'll get some technicians in here, anyway." He snapped his notebook shut.

"Lieutenant Chin," Nancy said, stopping him as he was about to return to the gallery. "Can you run a profile on Faith Arnold?"

"You think that's necessary?"

"She's been acting strangely," Nancy answered. She described the nervous behavior of the gallery owner and was glad to see the lieutenant nod his head.

"I'd planned on running one, anyway, but it's good to have your observations to confirm my hunch. I'm pretty sure I've seen her before." Then he asked Nancy for the name of her hotel so that he could call if he had any news of Emily.

"We'd really appreciate that, Lieutenant," Nancy said, and she went to rejoin the others.

Nancy, George, and Hannah made short work of saying goodbye to Faith Arnold. Glad to be free to leave the gallery, they walked out the front door. Peter Stine was close on their heels.

Nancy tried to ignore him. She walked briskly, despite Stine's efforts to get her to slow the pace and let George and Hannah move ahead of them. "We're concerned about our friend, Mr. Stine. I have a feeling you're not," she finally said.

"The big story here is the mob. And I'm warning you to keep your nose out of mob affairs. I've been digging around. Believe me, something is going to break in the next twenty-four hours, and you don't want to be in the middle of it."

"I'm only interested in finding Emily," Nancy assured him.

"Right. Well, I know where you *won't* find her—at the scene of this story. I plan to be the only reporter to cover this one, kid!" Stine abruptly broke away and turned back toward the gallery.

Nancy was glad to see him go. She grabbed Hannah's elbow and said, "Hannah, quick, can you go back to the restaurant across the street from the gallery? I want you to stay there, to keep an eye on Faith Arnold. George and I will come back later and meet you."

Hannah shook her head slowly. "I don't know, Nancy. I'm not sure I'm the best person for that. What if she leaves? I'm not as quick as you and George are."

"That's okay," replied Nancy. "Don't worry about following her. Just keep an eye on things. Watch who goes in and out of the gallery. See whether Faith Arnold leaves. If she does, note the time she comes back." Nancy patted Hannah on the shoulder and aimed her in the direction of the restaurant. "You'll be doing this for Emily, Hannah."

"Have a cup of tea or something," George suggested.

Hannah crossed the street. The girls watched until she entered the restaurant. Then Nancy led the way toward the nearby wharves. She slowed as they reached a row of little stores close to the waterfront, not quite sure what she was searching for.

Suddenly, Nancy touched George's arm, and the two came to a halt. Directly ahead of them was the balding man who had stolen Emily's camera two days before! He was leaving a store called Croft's Curio Shop.

Without a word, the girls began pursuing the thief, pretending to window shop as they followed him down the street. Moments later, two other men emerged from a doorway in front of the girls. They, too, moved down the street, behind the man, in front of Nancy and George.

Nancy paused when she realized that the men were not just tourists or businesspeople. They were also following the thief! With a chill, she recognized one of them: the cold-eyed man who had operated the crane on the wharf.

"George! One of those men is the crane operator!" Nancy exclaimed. "What could he want with that bald guy?"

Nancy and George pulled back a bit but continued to shadow the thief as he moved down the docks. They almost lost him once or twice when they had to stop to avoid being noticed by the crane operator and his friend. After several more blocks, the balding man stopped abruptly, forcing Nancy and George to duck into a doorway to escape being seen. When they emerged a moment later, they saw only the crane operator and his friend farther up the street. They were standing near several mountainous piles of packing crates and dustbins, looking confused. The balding man was nowhere to be seen.

"Looks like they've lost him," George said.

"Which means we've lost him, too." Nancy shook her head.

The girls watched as the men crossed the

street to a pay telephone. The grim crane operator put some coins into the slot and dialed a
number. Nancy and George darted through a
passageway between two storefronts, coming out
in an alley and stopping just behind the safety of
a trash dumpster. From there, they could hear
the man's phone conversation.

"We lost Blane," he reported in a flat voice.
Blane must be the balding man, but who *is* he?
Nancy wondered.

The crane operator spoke again, but he'd lowered his voice. Nancy leaned forward, trying to
hear.

". . . Silence someone . . . before it's too late."

Was Emily the one to be silenced? Nancy
wondered. The man sounded awfully angry. He
was apparently arguing with the person on the
other end of the phone. But the girls could not
make sense of the conversation.

Nancy narrowed her blue eyes, puzzling over
what she and George had heard. Was the man
referring to what had happened on the dock the
day before? Had she and Emily nearly been
killed because someone had to be silenced?

The girls heard the telephone receiver slam
down, and they slipped farther back into the
protection of the alley. From there, they saw the
two men walk away. The men seemed to be
arguing with each other. Nancy touched
George's wrist, indicating that they should stay
hidden until the men were safely gone.

"What did you make of that?" George whispered a few moments later.

"I'm not sure," Nancy replied. "It's very puzzling. And our bald thief—'Blane,' they called him—has gotten away from us again. But what part do those two play in all of this?"

Nancy was about to speculate further, when she heard a scraping sound behind her, the sound of shoe leather on the uneven surface of the alley. Before she could turn around, she and George heard another, far more terrifying sound: the unmistakable click of a gun being cocked. In the next instant, Nancy felt the touch of a cold steel pistol barrel on the back of her neck.

9

A Warning Too Late

"Turn around. Slowly," ordered a gruff voice.

Nancy and George did as they were told. They found themselves facing the wiry man they had seen watching outside Emily's apartment.

"Now," he said, "suppose you tell me who you are and what business you have with Emily Foxworth?" He puffed up his chest like a pit viper, but his tough-guy bravado didn't fool Nancy.

"We're friends of Emily's," she answered. "And we're very worried about her."

The man pulled the gun away from Nancy's head. "I'm an acquaintance of hers, too," he said. "My name's . . . Louie."

Nancy wasn't sure he was telling the truth, but

all she said was, "A friend who spies on her? Some friend."

"I wasn't spying. I was trying to get to her. Alone. Then you showed up. Twice!"

"Exactly what kind of acquaintance are you?" Nancy asked.

"Well . . . sometimes I help Emily."

"Help her? How?" George wanted to know.

"I guess you might call me an informant. Emily uses my—what shall I say?—my services sometimes when she's working on a crime story."

"Well, now she's missing," Nancy said sternly.

"I know. I saw. That's why I wanted to talk to you two. But first I had to make sure you weren't part of the mob."

"The mob? *Us?*" asked George incredulously.

"I've been trying to warn Emily," Louie went on.

"Warn her? About what?" asked Nancy.

"That she might be in danger."

"How did you know she might be in danger?"

"I can't tell you," he answered. "All I know is that it has something to do with information regarding the mob. I think she's got information that could be really dangerous for someone."

"But Emily doesn't know anything about the mob!" protested George.

"Louie," Nancy asked, "do you know if Emily's phone was bugged?"

"No idea." He shook his head.

"Look, you've got to do something for me, for Emily," Nancy said urgently. "See if you can find out what mob action is supposed to take place in the next twenty-four hours."

Louie laughed. "Do you know what you're asking? You must be crazy."

"I bet Emily could do you a big favor sometime, if you ever need one," Nancy pointed out. "She has an in at the police department. But she can't do you any favors unless we find her."

"Oh, brother," said Louie disgustedly.

Nancy ignored him. "We're staying at the—" she began.

"Never mind," Louie interrupted. "If I have to find you, I will. I've got my ways."

"I can see that," said Nancy, feeling slightly nervous. She wasn't sure she wanted to know about Louie's "ways."

"All right," Louie went on. "Any news I hear, I'll be in touch."

Nancy and George watched Louie disappear into the dark alley. They looked at each other. "Did that really happen?" George asked.

"I don't like him," said Nancy, shrugging. "But at least he's on our side. I mean, I think he is."

"Speaking of our side, we'd better get back to Hannah. She's just about the only person we know we can trust, and we've left her at the restaurant for a pretty long time. I don't think

70

she's too fond of this detective business, and I know she's upset about Emily."

Nancy looked at her watch. "You're right. It's late. Let's get Hannah and then go back to the hotel. I don't think there's anything else we can do tonight, anyway. Except hope Emily's all right."

George nodded in solemn agreement, and the two made their way back to the restaurant across from the gallery.

When the girls rejoined Hannah, they asked her if she wanted anything to eat. Hannah declined, saying she'd already eaten something with her tea. "I think we should return to the hotel in case Emily's kidnappers or the police call," she added.

Outside, Nancy hailed a passing cab, and on the silent ride to the hotel, she thought about the day's events. None of them made much sense to her. She wondered what—if anything—she could do to help find Emily.

The next morning, over an early breakfast in the hotel dining room, Nancy, Hannah, and George discussed what had happened the night before.

"Tell us again about what went on at the gallery after we left," Nancy suggested.

Hannah sighed, having been over this information several times the night before when they had returned to their hotel rooms. "Okay," said Hannah. "If you think it will help find Emily. Let's see, the journalist. What was his name?"

"Peter Stine," Nancy told her.

"Right. Well, after we left, he must have gone back. Because I saw him leave the gallery about fifteen minutes after I got to the restaurant. Then two men went in—one was carrying a camera. I think they were police officers. Then a woman in a big hat went in—and no, Nancy, I still can't describe her, because I couldn't see her face. Anyway, she only stayed in the gallery a minute. And that's all I saw."

"You're sure?" George asked.

"No, I'm not sure," Hannah replied testily. "You two were gone so long that I think I got punchy on all the tea I drank. I'm not sure of anything except that Emily's been kidnapped!" Tears filled Hannah's eyes.

"We'll find her," Nancy promised. She only hoped they would find her in time.

Later that morning, Lieutenant Chin stopped by the hotel to tell Nancy that so far the police had no leads on Emily's disappearance. "However, I found one bit of information I thought you'd be interested in," he added. "The computer printout on Faith Arnold shows a previous arrest record."

Nancy was intrigued. "For what?"

"Art scams. Falsely reporting artwork stolen,

collecting the insurance, and then selling the art on the black market."

George whistled.

"Was she prosecuted?" Nancy asked.

"There wasn't enough evidence to bring the case to court. She was released. The case was dropped."

"Lieutenant Chin, you'll keep us informed, won't you? You know how concerned we are about Emily," said Nancy seriously.

"I'll do what I can," he replied.

The three said goodbye to the lieutenant, and Hannah began to pace. "I'm so worried, girls," she said. "What if we never see her again?"

"Oh, Hannah, you can't think like that," cried Nancy. "Besides, Emily's pretty tough. Let's not give up on her so soon. I was thinking George and I should go over to her apartment and take another look around. Besides, I'm sure poor Tripod is hungry and lonesome. Do you have the key Emily gave you?"

"Yes," replied Hannah, fumbling in her purse for the key to Emily's apartment. "I think I should go, too," she added.

"It would be better if you stayed here, Hannah," Nancy said. "Lieutenant Chin or the kidnappers might decide to get in touch. Or even Emily herself."

Hannah's face fell. "I suppose you're right, Nancy. Okay. You two go over to the apartment. I'll wait for news. Good news, I hope."

73

Nancy hugged Hannah and urged her to hope for the best. Then she and George took the elevator to the lobby. When they stepped outside the hotel, a brisk breeze was blowing across Union Square. "Brrr," said Nancy, shivering.

"I guess this is the famous San Francisco wind they warned us about." George backed into the hotel doorway and huddled between the marble columns.

"I'll run back upstairs for our jackets," Nancy said, and she reentered the hotel. When she returned, she and George put on their jackets and braved the wind. "Shall we walk or take a taxi?" Nancy asked.

"Let's walk. I could use the exercise. But I wish I had thought to bring gloves."

"Me, too." Nancy stuffed her hands into her coat pockets for warmth. And her right hand closed over something that caused her to stop in her tracks.

"Nancy? What is it?" George studied her friend's face worriedly.

Nancy withdrew her hand from her pocket. She held out a roll of film.

"I don't get it," said George, looking at the film.

"This may be just what we've been looking for," Nancy said. "Or what the kidnappers have been looking for. This is the roll of film Emily asked me to hold at the airport. I forgot all about it. Come on. Let's get to Emily's and develop it. We don't have time to walk. We'll take a taxi."

The girls flagged a cab and gave the driver Emily's address. As the taxi sped along, they talked quietly.

"Do you remember what, if anything, Emily said was on this roll?" Nancy asked.

George frowned, trying to recall their first day in San Francisco.

"Didn't she say she had just come from China-town?" Nancy said. "That she'd been working on the 'Children of Change' story?"

"But why would anyone go to so much trouble for Emily's shots of cute kids? It doesn't make any sense, Nancy."

"No. Not unless—"

"Unless what?"

"Unless there's something else on this film. Something we don't know about."

"I wish we could tell the driver to hurry," George whispered, "like they do in the movies."

Five minutes later, they were standing in front of Emily's building, paying the cab fare. Nancy glanced up and down the street to make sure they weren't being watched. Then she led the way into the house.

The girls hurried up the stairs to Emily's apartment. But when they reached the door, Nancy pulled George back.

"What?" George asked.

"Shh. Listen." Nancy put her ear to the door. George leaned closer.

"All I hear is Tripod," George whispered.

"Exactly."

"So?"

Nancy's voice was barely above a whisper. "Remember? Emily said Tripod always talks up a storm when someone is around."

"You mean . . . ?"

Nancy nodded. "I think someone's in there."

"Hello there!" Tripod squawked. "Pretty bird. What a pretty bird!"

Cautiously, Nancy tried the door. The knob turned easily in her hand. And then it clicked open! The girls looked at each other. Someone was inside Emily's apartment. The question was, who?

10

The Buddha Clue

"Hello. Hello. Pretty boy. Awwrrk!" The parrot kept up his squawking as Nancy silently pushed open the door. The apartment was quiet, and with the noonday sun streaming in through the skylight and the windows, it seemed a cozy, unthreatening place.

George tugged gently at Nancy's elbow. "Are you sure we should go in if someone's here?" she whispered. She knew how many times the police had warned Nancy against entering a burglary scene if there was any chance the criminal might still be on the premises.

Nancy weighed her decision. "We have every right to be here, George. Whoever else is here does not. Unless it's Emily."

"I don't care how much right we have to be here," George retorted. "I'm not walking in on some intruder."

But Nancy stepped confidently into the room, and George followed, shutting the door behind them.

"Emily?" Nancy called, trying to sound cheerful and casual. "Are you home?"

The only answer came from Tripod. "Cake for Tripod. Cake for Tripod," he chattered.

"Hold on, bird," George told him. "We know you're hungry. We'll take care of you in a minute." Nancy gave George a grateful glance, realizing that although she was afraid, she was doing her best to act as if everything was normal.

The girls searched each room of the apartment. They saw nothing out of order. Nancy began to wonder if Tripod was just talking from loneliness and hunger. Or maybe he'd somehow heard the girls before they reached the door of the apartment. But why had the apartment been unlocked? "All right," she said. "Let's hit the darkroom."

Nancy opened the door to the darkroom—and screamed.

Peter Stine stepped out, a small smile on his lips. "Were you expecting Emily, girls?" he asked them.

"We weren't expecting *you*," Nancy said. She took a deep breath. "What are you doing here?"

"Yeah," George spoke up from behind Nancy,

78

trying to sound tough. "What are you doing here?"

Stine didn't answer. Instead, he turned to unhook his jacket from the back of the darkroom door.

"Look around, ladies," he said pleasantly. "You won't find anything missing or damaged."

"You know, you have a lot of nerve, breaking into Emily's apartment," Nancy said.

Stine shouldered his jacket and picked up his camera case, which was on the floor of the darkroom. "Let's just say I know Emily is on to the same story I am."

"That's no reason to break into her apartment," said George, unable to hide her anger.

"Listen," Stine said, turning suddenly on the girls and pointing his finger at them. "I won't let that woman steal my thunder on this story." He closed the door of the darkroom and strode into the living room.

Nancy watched him for a moment, gambling with what to say next. "Mr. Stine," she finally began, "how can Emily Foxworth get in your way if she's missing?"

Stine ignored her. He had reached the front door.

"Or is Emily missing so that she *can't* get in your way?" Nancy pressed.

Peter Stine yanked the door open, then spun around to face Nancy. His craggy face was flushed. "I had no part in kidnapping Emily

79

Foxworth, and you're crazy if you think I did! She was probably taken because she knew something she shouldn't have known." He yanked the door open and walked out without closing it behind him.

Nancy followed him as far as the doorway. "I'm going to find Emily, Mr. Stine. No matter what!"

But Peter Stine didn't answer. He ran down the stairs. Nancy heard the front door slam.

"He doesn't seem too worried about Emily," George commented when Nancy reentered the living room.

"No. That's what bugs me, George. Why isn't he at least pretending to care about her?" Nancy stared into space, bewildered by Stine, wondering what he was up to.

"Do you think we ought to call the police?" George asked.

"Later. Right now, let's see if we can figure out what that man was doing here. Then we've got to develop Emily's film."

A thorough search of the darkroom revealed nothing out of order. It looked just the way it had looked the day before when Nancy and Emily had tidied it after the break-in. Whether he had searched or stolen or replaced something, Stine had certainly been careful to leave no sign that he'd been there.

Nancy went briskly about the business of setting up the chemicals necessary to develop the

80

roll of film. Then, using a light-proof work bag, she loaded the exposed film into the canister. After checking the temperature on the chemicals, Nancy poured a solution into the canister.

While they waited for the film to dry, the girls made a quick lunch for themselves in Emily's kitchen and fed Tripod some bird seed. When they returned to the darkroom, Nancy turned out the light and made a proof sheet from the black-and-white negatives. Then she and George pored over the tiny images, looking for clues.

"They're just what Emily said they were," George observed. "Pictures of city children. Nothing suspicious here."

Nancy bent over the proof sheet. "I don't know. Take a close look at that one. The background looks interesting. I want to enlarge it."

Nancy set up the enlarger for the new print and turned out the light again. Yes, there was plenty of detail in the background of the shot. She exposed a sheet of photographic paper and ran it through the chemicals to develop, impatient now with the time it would take for the image to emerge and then set.

Finally, the print was ready to rinse. Nancy shook the extra water from the photo and picked it up for a closer look.

George looked, too. "It's just some kids on fishing boats, Nancy. It looks like the older ones are working and the little ones are playing around."

Nancy searched for a magnifying glass and found one in a drawer. She held the glass over a corner of the print.

"Wait, Nancy! Isn't that Blane?" cried George. "You know, the bald guy?"

"You mean the one getting off the boat, next to that bearded man?"

"Yes. Isn't that him?"

"Could be, I guess." Nancy stared for a moment at Blane, then focused more closely on the bearded man. "This one," she said, "the one with the chain around his neck—" Nancy paused, then caught her breath. "George, that's an ivory Buddha on the chain! Just like the one Harold Kesack used to wear. Remember Emily's award-winning photo?"

"But I thought he was dead," George said.

"So did I. Emily told us he died in a plane crash five years ago, right? She ought to know." Nancy set the print on the counter and turned to empty the processing trays and put away the chemicals. George helped her straighten up the darkroom. Then they returned to the print, studying it as if it held the key to Emily's kidnapping.

Nancy continued to stare at the photo of the bearded man. "Let's compare it to the shot Emily already has."

"But this picture was taken just a few days ago, Nancy. Kesack's been dead for five years."

"I know, but it's so strange to see that Buddha on two different people. Let's check."

The girls took the print into the living room, only to be confronted by the blank space on the wall. Nancy shook her head. "I forgot about the burglary." She sighed as she remembered the missing photos. "The *first* burglary, that is," she added. "Well, maybe we can find the negative. Come on." They headed back to the darkroom.

It took the girls several minutes to figure out Emily's files. Although they were neatly organized, it was clear that Emily's filing system was hers alone and that she didn't expect anyone else to need to find things for her. It took fifteen minutes for Nancy to locate the section that held the negatives from five years before.

She leafed through the folders, looking for one that might contain images of Kesack. At last, she came to a space where three or four file folders had been removed.

"George, I think those negatives must be out of order or filed somewhere else. There's a big gap here. Entire months are missing, then the next year begins, and so far no shots of Kesack."

"This is like looking for a needle in a haystack, Nancy," said George. "Plus, it's depressing."

"Depressing is right." Nancy shook her head, then abruptly closed the negative files. "Well, anyway, we've got this shot from a few days ago, and it sure looks like the same Buddha I remember. Maybe Emily does know Blane, if he worked with Kesack. She said she remembered seeing a man like Blane somewhere before. That would explain it. But I just don't see how these pieces of the mystery fit together."

"Yeah, Kesack is dead," said George wearily.

"And his picture has been stolen from the wall."

"And Emily isn't here to help us find the negatives."

"But—" Nancy paused. She walked out of the darkroom, taking the photo with her. George followed her into the kitchen, almost bumping into Nancy when she turned suddenly to face her. "But," Nancy said again in a low voice, "maybe that's just what we're supposed to think."

"What?"

"That Kesack is dead. Maybe he's not."

The girls stared at each other for a moment. Then they grabbed their jackets. Tripod squawked.

"See you later, bird!" called George. "We'll come back to feed you again."

The girls closed and locked the apartment door, then clattered down the stairs.

"So, what's next?" George asked, glad to be outdoors again. She quickened her pace to match Nancy's long stride.

"We'd better get this photo to Lieutenant Chin," Nancy replied.

"What good do you think it will do?"

"I don't know, but Chin's the only one we might be able to trust. Besides, I want to tell him about Peter Stine."

As the girls stood at the corner watching for a cruising cab, Nancy wondered what it might mean if Kesack were still alive. The thought chilled her.

"George," she said, "if Kesack, who's one of the most dangerous crime bosses ever, is still alive and in San Francisco—" She stopped talking long enough to climb into the taxi that pulled over for them. "Police headquarters," she told the cabbie.

"What, Nancy?" George prodded her.

Nancy looked soberly at George. "If he's really here," she continued, "then I don't think a single one of us is truly safe!"

11

Little Shop of Danger

It was early evening by the time Nancy and George left the police station. They sat on the steps outside the building and talked. The breeze that had been blowing so briskly earlier in the day had calmed, and now a light fog was moving in across the bay.

"Finally, we had something concrete to give Lieutenant Chin," Nancy said with satisfaction. "Let's see what he can do with the photo. Maybe now something important will break."

"He promised to investigate Kesack's plane crash and death. That's important," George pointed out.

"That's also five years ago. Coming up with information soon is going to be pretty difficult. I guess right now there's not much we can do but wait and see what's uncovered," Nancy said. "In the meantime, I was thinking that a visit to Faith Arnold might not be a bad idea. I want to talk to her about this art scam business. Maybe she knows something about Emily's abduction, something she's not telling anyone."

The girls made their way across town to the art gallery. The hushed museumlike atmosphere once again struck Nancy as they stepped onto the plush carpeting that muffled their footsteps.

They found Faith Arnold seated at her desk in an attractively furnished office at the rear of the building. Nancy noted that a great deal of money had been spent decorating the room. The desk Faith Arnold sat behind was obviously an antique. Chinese, Nancy guessed, looking at the legs, carved to look like fierce dragons.

"Ms. Arnold?" Nancy said, pausing in the doorway.

The gallery owner glanced up, and recognition flashed in her eyes. Nancy moved forward, giving her no chance to retreat. George remained in the doorway.

"We'd like to talk to you about Emily Foxworth and her missing photographs," Nancy said.

"You have no business barging in here like this. I've already told the police everything I know." Faith Arnold glared at the two girls.

"Are you sure, Ms. Arnold?" Nancy thought the woman looked awfully worried.

"Of course I'm sure. I'm as troubled by Emily Foxworth's abduction as you are."

"Perhaps there's something you left out or forgot," Nancy said coaxingly. "Why don't you tell us how you're involved in this situation."

"I have no intention of telling you anything. And I'm not involved. Now please leave."

"Are you aware that the police already suspect you?" Nancy went on.

Faith Arnold stood up. "Why would they suspect me?" she snapped.

"Because you've had problems with them before," George answered.

"How do you know about that?"

"We've been doing some investigating ourselves," Nancy replied. "Now, won't you tell us *exactly* what you know? Your only chance is to help us."

Faith Arnold sank back down in her chair.

"Who kidnapped Emily?" asked Nancy.

"I don't know. Honest."

Nancy took a gamble. "What relationship does a man named Blane have to Harold Kesack?"

"Harold Kesack? The mob ringleader? But he's dead!"

Nancy leaned forward. "So you *do* know Harold Kesack."

"Oh, everyone knows about that," she replied. "It was in all the papers. Anyway, Kesack's dead. I've only had dealings with Arnie Blane."

"How does he fit into the picture?"

Faith Arnold sighed. "Blane used to work for Kesack. He told me he wanted Emily's photos. He threatened to expose my police record if I didn't give them to him."

"Did he say why he wanted the pictures?" George asked.

"No."

"The pictures Emily went looking for just before she disappeared—did Blane already have them?" Nancy wanted to know.

"Yes. I'd taken them out of her portfolio. But you have to understand. I've been trying to go straight. I have a nice business here. Good clientele. I wanted nothing to do with Blane."

"We saw this Arnie Blane leaving Croft's Curio Shop. Do you know anything about that store?"

Faith Arnold sighed again, then answered wearily, "I've heard Croft's a smuggler. That's all I know."

"That's all?"

"Well, I've also heard that Croft can get *anything* in or out of the country."

Nancy paused, thinking. "Do the numbers 37-4-11-12 mean anything to you?"

"No. Listen, whatever happens, I want you to know I feel terrible about Emily. She's one of my favorite artists. And people like her work."

"If Blane contacts you again, I suggest you call the police immediately," Nancy told her. "It would be in your best interest."

Several moments later, Nancy and George left

the art gallery. "We'll unravel this mess. I know we will," George said as they walked outside.

"Let's go to the curio shop. Maybe our unraveling will start there," suggested Nancy.

"We don't have much to go on."

"No, but now at least we found out that Blane worked for Kesack. For all we know, Kesack's still alive, maybe even somewhere in the city—with Emily. But what does he want with her?"

"Beats me. And what about those two men we saw following Blane? How do the crane operator and his buddy fit into all of this?"

Nancy and George mused over the confusing details of the case as they made their way to Croft's. On the corner near the shop, they stopped at a phone booth to call Hannah.

"No word yet, Nancy," Hannah reported, "and I'm very worried. But what's worse is that I feel so useless. I want to *do* something to help find Emily."

"The most useful thing you can do right now is to sit tight, Hannah," Nancy said gently. "Have you eaten anything?"

"Yes. I called room service. And I'm watching TV when I'm not staring at the phone, willing it to ring."

Hannah sounded so lost. Nancy wanted to comfort her. But she knew the only way to do that was to find Emily. "George and I are going to check out a few more leads," she said, "and then we'll be back in touch."

"Just be careful, Nancy. You don't know who you're dealing with. They might be very dangerous. In fact, we know they are." Fear sounded in Hannah's voice.

"Try not to worry, Hannah. You know George and I will be careful," Nancy said. "Just stay by the phone, okay?"

Hannah promised to do so, and Nancy hung up.

"Well?" asked George hopefully.

"Nothing yet," replied Nancy. She and George continued down the street. As they approached the curio shop, Nancy had an idea. "Let's try taking a look around back."

The girls made sure no one was watching them, then ducked into a side alley. It was more like a narrow street that continued beyond the end of the curio shop building to the next street. Cautiously, they sneaked behind the building. The front had been remodeled as part of a street renovation project, but the rear of the building was old, dilapidated, and ready to crumble. As the girls rounded a corner, the back door of Croft's opened. Nancy yanked George into the shadows of the alley. Peering around the corner, the girls watched two men leave the store. They were the same two men Nancy and George had followed earlier, the men who had been trailing Blane! The girls moved a little way back down the alley, ready to run if the men came that way. They didn't. Nancy and George watched, relieved, as the pair headed up the alley in the opposite direction. "George," Nancy whispered, "you follow them, and be careful. I'm going into the shop."

"All right." George ran after the two men, while Nancy crept to the back door of the curio shop. Discovering that it was ajar, she tiptoed in.

Croft's was a small store that seemed to sell mostly souvenirs—ashtrays shaped like San Francisco Bay, sweatshirts, postcards, and mugs. T-shirts were stacked floor to ceiling. Dusty children's toys and animals made out of seashells were displayed on dirty counters.

Nancy found a room marked "Office" and paused to listen. When she heard nothing, she pushed on the door. It swung open. The room was vacant. She wondered where the owner of the shop was. It *was* late, and most of the stores in the neighborhood were closed by then, but why had the back door been open?

When Nancy's eyes adjusted to the dim light, she saw that the office had been trashed, as if the two previous visitors had been looking for something—something important. Papers littered the floor. The desk drawers had been pulled out and their contents scattered. What had the two men been looking for? Nancy wondered.

She noticed a ledger on the desk and discovered that several of its pages had been torn out. The writing in the ledger looked familiar. She'd seen it before. But where? Thoughtfully, she pulled from her pocket the scrap of paper with the numbers written on it that she'd found on Emily's floor. She compared the awkward scrawl to the pages in the ledger. The writing appeared to match! Nancy removed a ledger page for herself and stuffed it in her pocket.

With the new evidence in hand, Nancy was about to depart when she heard someone enter the shop. She ducked behind a pile of T-shirts. When she peeked out cautiously, a man she'd never seen before was entering the office. When he saw the mess, he muttered something angrily. Then Nancy heard him pick up the phone and dial a number. "It's Croft," he said in a harsh whisper a few moments later. "Someone's been in here . . . Yeah, the whole office. The place is a mess . . . Okay . . . Okay. I'll be right there."

Nancy took her cue and ran out the back door just as Croft hung up the phone. She pounded through the alley, turning often to look over her shoulder—and bumped into a figure standing near the street.

The figure gasped. "You scared me half to death!" George exclaimed.

"*You* scared *me!* What are you doing here, anyway?"

"I lost the men," George answered ruefully. "I was on my way back."

"Well, let's get out of here. Croft's in the store, and he's on his way out."

93

The two girls dashed onto the main street. When they felt safe again and could see neither Croft nor the other men, Nancy told George what she'd seen in the shop.

"I don't think they do much business," she added. "At least not souvenir business. Most of the merchandise hasn't been dusted in years. That place is a front, George. Probably for the smuggling operation Faith Arnold mentioned. Anyway, look what I found."

Nancy pulled out the page from the ledger and the scrap of paper with the numbers on it and showed them to George. "What do you think?"

"The writing's the same!"

"That's what I thought, too. But what the connection is, I don't know. So tell me what happened when you tried to follow the crane operator and that other guy."

"They went up the alley and then just got into a limo and drove away. I think it might have been the same car Emily was kidnapped in."

"Could you see the license plate numbers?" asked Nancy.

"Nope. They were covered with mud. I couldn't read them."

"I don't know how much that means . . . Which direction was it headed?"

"Downtown."

"You know, I have a funny feeling we'd better get back to the art gallery, George. And fast. Those guys just might be interested in getting rid of anyone who knows anything about Kesack or Blane. Faith Arnold could be in real danger."

The two girls rushed back to the art gallery, Nancy's brain working overtime. If Kesack was still alive and the two men worked for him, why had they been following Blane? And why had they searched Croft's office? It didn't make any sense—yet.

When Nancy and George arrived at the gallery, panting and out of breath, they found the front door unlocked and the place in darkness. "Ms. Arnold?" Nancy called.

The girls ran to the office. "Ms. Arnold!" Nancy called again.

George was first through the door. She stopped, shocked by the grisly sight in front of her. "Nancy," she said shakily. "Faith Arnold's been hurt. Badly."

12

The Golden Gate Trap

While George phoned the police, Nancy tried unsuccessfully to rouse Faith Arnold by calling her name and rubbing her hands. When she took her pulse she found it weak but steady. "A good sign," Nancy said to herself. Then she found a coat in the office and covered the woman to help keep her warm until medical help arrived. Only when she thought she'd done everything possible did she happen to look around the office. The room was in chaos.

Just minutes after George made the phone call, the police arrived, and an ambulance pulled up in front of the gallery. Then Lieutenant Chin showed up. He followed the paramedics as they rolled the stretcher bearing the still-unconscious

Faith Arnold through the gallery and out the door. He listened intently as one of the paramedics told him that Ms. Arnold had received severe head injuries.

Chin shook his head. "Whoever broke into the gallery meant business," he told Nancy.

The lieutenant turned to talk with his officers, and the ambulance rushed Faith Arnold off to the emergency room. After a moment, Chin signaled to Nancy and George. "What made you girls come by the gallery tonight?" he asked them quietly.

Nancy realized she hadn't told the lieutenant about the encounter she and George had had with Louie, or about the men who had followed Arnie Blane from Croft's shop. She thought about volunteering this information and decided against it. She was reluctant, too, to tell him just yet about having been in Croft's vandalized shop.

"We were out for a walk near the wharves, and we spotted a limousine that looked like the one Emily was kidnapped in. Two men were inside, and they looked familiar, too," Nancy said.

"So," George added, catching on, "we tried to follow the car and realized it was headed this way."

"We just jumped to the conclusion that Faith Arnold might be in trouble if she were in the gallery alone," Nancy finished, truthfully.

The lieutenant thought for a moment, tapping

his pencil against his pocket notebook. "Good thinking," he said at last. "For Ms. Arnold's sake, I'm glad you got here as soon as you did." Then he directed his men to check the gallery for evidence that might help establish why the owner had been attacked.

Nancy led them to the office and pointed out the chaos. The office had been thoroughly ransacked. Drawers were upside down on the floor, their contents scattered. A couple of artists' portfolios had been ripped open. A cascade of original artwork, prints, and photos had been rifled through and lay in a heap on the floor.

"Whew! What a mess! I hope Ms. Arnold has insurance," Chin said.

The police team finished checking out the gallery, office, and storeroom, and Nancy was puzzled that no clues were found. Several of Emily's photos had been taken from the wall but lay discarded on the floor.

Nancy looked more closely at the photographs. They were pictures Emily had shot on the docks or in Chinatown. From the clothing styles, Nancy judged they had been taken within the last few years. She couldn't spot any people or themes in them that seemed unusual.

"I guess that's it." The lieutenant's voice startled Nancy from her thoughts. "The back door was open. They must have broken in and caught Ms. Arnold by surprise." He added that he and his men were wrapping up their investigation for the evening. "We'll seal the gallery until Ms. Arnold's condition is determined," he said.

Lieutenant Chin turned to speak to one of the officers, then turned back to Nancy and George. "I'll bet you've done enough running for one day. Why don't I drop you off at your hotel?" he offered kindly.

"That would be great. Thank you," the girls answered at once, glad they wouldn't have to stand on the dark street, waiting for a taxi.

On the way back to the hotel, Nancy was quiet, puzzling over the new developments. Her visit to San Francisco was definitely not turning out to be the lazy, leisurely vacation she and George and Hannah had planned. And they had seen a side of San Francisco they hadn't expected to find: a dark, dangerous side.

Nancy thought again about the slip of paper in her pocket, the one she had found in Emily's apartment. What was the connection between the cryptic numbers and the matching handwriting in the ledger in Croft's Curio Shop? *Was* there any connection? Maybe the handwriting belonged to one of the kidnappers. Had one of the break-ins at Emily's apartment actually been a kidnapping attempt? Nancy closed her eyes and shook her head impatiently. She was glad to see the hotel up ahead and thought longingly of her bed.

Lieutenant Chin brought his sedan to a stop at the canopy leading to the front entrance of the hotel. "I'll be in touch if there are any new developments," he promised. He climbed out and opened the passenger door for the girls.

"Thank you, Lieutenant Chin," Nancy replied. She and George headed wearily up the hotel steps. The uniformed doorman, younger than the one who had been on duty earlier, smiled at the tired girls as he held the door open for them.

"Big day of sightseeing?" he asked with a smile.

George laughed. "Um, revisiting familiar sights, I guess you could call it."

Hannah was glad to see Nancy and George. She'd become anxious as the afternoon had stretched into evening and still there had been no word of Emily, and the girls hadn't called back. "I was beginning to wonder if you'd been kidnapped, too!" Hannah exclaimed.

"Close, but happily, no." George smiled.

"Hannah, I'm sorry you worried about us." Nancy apologized as she and George dropped gratefully onto an overstuffed couch. Nancy pulled off her shoes and started to tell Hannah about the experiences she and George had had since their late-afternoon phone call.

"Wait a minute," Hannah interrupted. "You two must be sick—have you taken your temperatures lately?"

"What?" George looked at Nancy in confusion.

"Dinner! Have you forgotten about food? No matter how serious things are, you've got to eat."

Nancy suddenly realized that she was starving.

"Shall we order room service?" George asked.

"No," Hannah said quickly. "I'd like to go out. And there's—well, I doubt if it's one of the famous places Emily would have chosen," Hannah said softly, "but I did notice a little restaurant about two blocks away. It looked nice enough. Shall we try it?" She picked up her pocketbook and moved toward the door. Nancy put on her shoes, and the girls readily followed. Within moments, the three of them were walking through the cool evening.

Soon, refreshed by their meal, Nancy and George finished updating Hannah on the events of the day. Hannah listened intently at first but then became restless.

"I want to go back to the hotel. I want to be there in case there's news about Emily. Do you realize she's been gone twenty-four hours now, with no word?"

Nancy nodded in sympathy. "You're right, Hannah. We should get back. Lieutenant Chin promised to call us if there was any news."

The three were walking through the hotel lobby when the bell captain called Nancy over to the registration desk. He handed her a slip of

101

paper. "You just got a phone call," he told her. "The man wouldn't leave his name, but he left a number for you to call."

"Thank you," said Nancy, and she ran to catch up with the others at the elevator. When they reached their rooms, Nancy made a dash for the telephone. She dialed quickly and was relieved when her call was answered almost immediately.

"Yes?" said a cautious male voice. "Who is it?"

"This is Nancy Drew," Nancy said calmly, shifting her gaze from the faces of her friends to the old-fashioned dial on the telephone.

There was a brief pause. Then the voice said, "I have information about Emily Foxworth's disappearance."

"Will you tell me where to find her?"

"The info might," was the brief answer. "If you want information about Emily, you'll have to meet me. Alone."

Nancy thought the voice sounded familiar. "Is this Louie?" she asked.

"Never mind who it is. If you want to learn about Foxworth, you'll have to do as I say and meet me."

"All right. When and where?"

"The Golden Gate Bridge, alone. Meet me on the pedestrian walkway, halfway across. And be there by ten P.M." The man hung up the telephone. Nancy listened to the steady buzz on the line.

She turned to smile at her friends as she

replaced the receiver. "Well, I guess I'll get an unexpected view of the Golden Gate tonight!"

George and Hannah, having heard only Nancy's half of the conversation, hovered nearby, eager to hear what she'd learned. Nancy started to repeat the conversation, then glanced at her watch.

"Uh-oh. It's nearly nine-thirty, and I have to be there by ten."

"What?" Hannah was startled to see Nancy reach for her jacket and stuff her wallet into one of the pockets.

"I have to meet him on the Golden Gate Bridge by ten."

"Alone?" George was alarmed. She was used to Nancy and her adventures—but not to risky trips alone at night.

"I think it was Louie," Nancy said, trying to reassure them that she would be all right.

"I really don't think you ought to go alone, Nancy," Hannah said sternly.

"Me neither." George thought for a moment. "Maybe I could go with you and stay hidden."

"No. He said for me to come alone."

"But we don't know for sure that it was Louie. And even if it was, we don't know if we can trust him. Nancy, what if *he's* not alone?" George looked unusually worried.

"I've got to go. This might be our only chance to find Emily. Don't worry. I'll be careful." Nancy shrugged on her jacket and ran to the door, turning back as she opened it. "I'll be just fine," she told George and Hannah.

Downstairs, Nancy spoke to the young bell captain while she waited for a taxi. She noticed that the fog was thickening and shivered as a chill ran down her spine. But when a taxi pulled up, Nancy told the woman at the wheel to take her to the famous old bridge.

"You going there alone, honey? I don't think that's a very good idea." The driver didn't hesitate to give Nancy another piece of her mind when Nancy requested that she stop the cab near Fort Point, where the pedestrian walkway began. As Nancy paid her fare, the driver protested again. "Maybe I should wait until you've come back. Or, if you want, I could meet you on the other side."

"I'm not sure whether I'll be going all the way across. But don't worry." Nancy smiled at the concerned woman.

"Well, even a tourist spot isn't safe at this hour of the night," the cabbie said. "You be careful."

"I will. Thanks." Nancy turned and headed for the walkway. It was dark, except for the lights of the bridge and the stream of headlights from the traffic flowing along below.

Nancy glanced at her wristwatch—nearly ten. She'd have to hurry if she wanted to get to the center of the bridge in time. One of the tourist brochures she'd seen had mentioned the length of the bridge. Nancy had forgotten the figure, but as she strode along the fog-dampened concrete, she was willing to believe that the bridge was at least a mile long.

The water far below was black, and Nancy thought it looked very cold. She admired the strength of the huge girders and made a mental note to bring George and Hannah—and Emily— back to the bridge for some photos before the end of their vacation.

The fog was growing even thicker. Nancy glanced back over her shoulder. She couldn't see the end of the bridge. Soon it would be difficult to see more than a few yards in any direction.

These aren't the best circumstances for a late-night rendezvous, she thought unhappily, pulling the collar of her warm jacket more closely around her neck. She wondered again whether she could trust Louie, or whether it was even Louie who had called. A few more paces brought her to what must surely have been the center of the bridge. Nancy checked her watch, very aware of being the only person within sight on the walk-way. It was exactly ten o'clock.

She breathed a sigh of relief when she heard footsteps.

But then she tensed. The footsteps were heavy. She couldn't imagine thin, wiry Louie making such a sound. And the footsteps were coming from both sides. Suddenly, out of the fog, two men appeared. It didn't take her long to see that, under the dark hats and heavy overcoats, they were the same two thugs who'd been trailing Arnie Blane! Louie was nowhere in sight. Neither was anyone else.

Nancy greeted the men calmly. "Do you have the information about Emily Foxworth?" she asked.

One of the men growled something unintelligible in the harsh voice Nancy had last heard the day she and George had hidden in the alley and listened in on the mysterious phone call.

Nancy turned then to the thin-faced man and shuddered as she remembered how coldly he had sat in the cab of his crane on the docks.

"I was promised information on Emily Foxworth," Nancy went on, sounding far more calm than she felt.

"Were you?" The crane operator had not become any more pleasant since their last encounter.

"Which one of you did I speak with on the phone?" Nancy asked, trying to figure out what to do.

"Never mind that." The other man brushed aside her question. "Do you know how many people have jumped from this bridge, sweetheart?"

"I came for information about Emily Foxworth," Nancy repeated. "If you don't have anything to tell me, I'll go back to the hotel."

The crane operator moved slowly toward her.

"You know all those poor people who jumped

from this bridge, kid?" the other man went on. "Well, you're about to become one of them." He lunged for her.

These men are killers, Nancy thought, but I'm not about to become their next victim! She jerked away from the man—and ran into the other one.

"Why don't you save us a whole lot of trouble?" asked the crane operator.

Nancy looked around frantically. She was trapped, with a killer on each side and the freezing waters of San Francisco Bay hundreds of feet below.

13

The Broken Code

Nancy made a split-second decision to vault over the railing into the oncoming traffic. It's my only choice, she thought. But before she could move, the men closed in on her, cutting off her escape route. Nancy glanced behind her. The water in the bay below was not something she wanted to think about.

The men drew closer. And in a flash, Nancy made her move. She jumped up and pulled herself onto the girder above her head. The crane operator grabbed for her foot, and Nancy's tennis shoe came off in his hand but she couldn't worry about that. She scrambled along the girder.

"Where is she?" she heard one of the men ask.

108

"I don't know. It's too foggy. I can't see a thing."

"She's got to be around here somewhere. We can't let her get away."

Silently, Nancy crept along the girder until she found a place where she could drop back onto the walkway. Once there, she vaulted over the side to the next level. Her landing was loud enough to alert the men.

"Down there, Joe. I heard something."

But Nancy's lean, younger body gave her a distinct advantage over her pursuers.

"I can't believe you let her get away," she heard the crane operator say disgustedly.

Nancy ran out into the mass of slow-moving cars, dodging between the vehicles. The fog was heavy but definitely to her advantage. She could hear the two men behind her but knew they were having trouble seeing her. However, dodging both the traffic and the thugs was no simple matter.

Nancy decided to run straight through the onslaught of vehicles. "Hey, whatcha doin'?" a man yelled at her. He honked his horn.

Nancy listened and suddenly became aware that her two followers had split up and were coming at her from opposite directions. Once again, she had to make a quick decision. By jumping at the last possible moment between two cars, she managed to escape. But the second car barely missed hitting her.

"Watch out!" the driver yelled.

A horn blared, and a van rear-ended the car that had almost hit Nancy. The owners of both vehicles jumped out and began to argue.

"I couldn't help it," Nancy heard one driver say. "There was a girl in my way."

"Sure there was, Mister. There was a unicorn, too."

The voices faded as Nancy darted along the side of the roadway. She used the moment of confusion to her advantage. A pickup truck going in the direction away from the accident slowed down to take a look at the situation. Nancy quickly jumped over the barrier dividing the lanes of traffic, hoisted herself up, and climbed into the back. Then she flattened herself against the bed of the truck. And just in time. She heard heavy footsteps run and was sure they belonged to one of her pursuers. Nancy held her breath and willed herself to become invisible.

The footsteps stopped right behind the truck.

"I think we've lost her," Nancy heard a voice say.

"How could we have lost her? Someone's going to pay for this one, Joe. And I think it's us. Come on. Let's keep looking. She's got to be around here somewhere."

"Yeah. Hey, maybe she got into one of these cars."

Nancy felt the fear return. Her heart began to

pound, and perspiration ran down her back despite the fact that it was quite cold outside.

Just then, she felt the comforting lurch of the truck starting. It wasn't until the vehicle was moving at a steady pace that she felt her heart slow down. That one was too close for comfort, she told herself.

Nancy crouched in the back of the truck and forced herself to breathe deeply. After several minutes, she dared to peek out the back of the truck and take a look at her surroundings. She recognized the Presidio army base she had passed the day she went in search of Peter Stine.

Soon she felt a lurching motion and heard the gears of the truck grinding, a certain indication that the truck was now in stop-and-go traffic, which meant traffic lights, which meant she was back in the city.

When the truck halted once again, Nancy took another peek outside. The truck was nearing the wharf district. Here the traffic thinned. She made up her mind. This was her best bet. As soon as the truck slowed for the next stop light, she would jump out.

The wait seemed endless. Finally, Nancy felt the vehicle slow and then heard the sound of the driver down-shifting the gears. It was time.

The driver of the car behind the truck beeped his horn when he saw Nancy jump from the rear of the pickup truck. His lights momentarily blinded Nancy.

She turned away, waited for her vision to clear, and then tried to determine just where she was. Suddenly, Nancy realized something. Something important. She hoped her discovery would shed some light on the case.

What she needed now, she decided, was a phone. The search for one took her running down a lonely, narrow street. It was a place of bustle and high activity during the day, but at night it was a no-man's land.

Nancy ran for two long blocks before she found a telephone.

She dialed the hotel. "George, it's me."

"Nancy, are you all right? Hannah and I have been worried sick. I was about to call the police."

"I'm fine. I'll tell you all about it later. I don't have time right now. Can you and Hannah meet me right away? It's important."

"Of course. Where are you?"

Nancy explained to George how to find her.

"We'll be there as soon as possible," George assured her.

"Thanks. We don't have much time."

Nancy was pacing impatiently when, twenty minutes later, George and Hannah arrived in a cab.

"This is kind of a creepy area, Nancy," Hannah said nervously. "The cabbie kept saying, 'Are you sure you want to get out here?'"

"I know, Hannah. But this is important. Listen. I think I understand now what the numbers on

112

the slip of paper stand for. It hit me as I was running along the wharves after I jumped out of the pickup truck."

"Pickup truck? What pickup truck?" George asked.

"I'll tell you later," Nancy said. "Anyway, the wharves are numbered. The wharf where Emily and I were almost hit by the crates is thirty-seven!"

"Let me see that paper," George said. Nancy pulled the worn scrap from the pocket of her jeans. "Fits," George agreed. "But what about the other numbers?"

Hannah suddenly looked at Nancy sternly. "Young lady, you're missing a shoe! What did you do with your other one? Imagine, running around without a shoe."

"I'll tell you about that later, too, Hannah," Nancy said hurriedly.

"What about the other numbers?" George asked again. "Four, eleven, and twelve?"

"Four-eleven just might stand for today's date, April eleventh."

"Let me guess," Hannah said. "And the twelve is the time. Right?"

"I hope so." Nancy looked at her watch. "And if it is, we have only about an hour to find Emily before something big happens."

"Then let's get going!" George exclaimed.

"I'm all for that," Hannah agreed.

"I think you'd be most helpful, Hannah, if you

113

called Lieutenant Chin to tell him what we've learned. Convince him that he should get here as quickly as possible. If I'm right about this, we're going to be needing all the help we can get." Nancy swiveled her head. "I saw a—yes, there it is." She pointed to a lighted sign, "24-Hour Diner," about a block away. "You can make the call and wait for Lieutenant Chin there, Hannah. Do you want us to walk—"

"No," Hannah interrupted. "I can do it—for Emily." She gave each girl a brief hug and walked briskly away.

The two girls headed for wharf thirty-seven and began searching.

They walked around the outsides of the warehouses that fronted the wharf. All were locked up for the night, and security guards were posted in front of several. The girls cautiously avoided being seen by them.

"No need to let anyone know we're here," Nancy whispered to George from the shadows.

Because time was running out, the girls decided to separate when they reached the last warehouse on the wharf. They would investigate the building from opposite directions.

"Meet you back here in five minutes," George said to Nancy. "If one of us doesn't return on time, the other will go looking for her, okay?"

Nancy nodded in agreement. Then she set off. She noted that this storage building was similar to the others they had checked. Huge sliding doors on the dock side of the building allowed for easy loading and unloading of goods. She saw no windows and no other doors in the warehouse.

The girls met at their appointed spot in less than three minutes. "Well?" George asked.

"Nothing," Nancy said glumly. "What about you?"

"The same."

"I wish I knew what we were looking for."

"Even *where* to look would be a step in the right direction."

Just then, Nancy noticed a figure approaching the warehouse entrance. She nudged George, and the girls pressed themselves into the shadows.

"Could be just a security guard on his rounds," George whispered.

Nancy shrugged. From the safety of their hiding place, they continued to watch. The figure disappeared in the darkness and then was illuminated for a moment by a streetlight. The figure, a man, turned, glanced around, and was swallowed up by the blackness.

George and Nancy looked at each other, disbelief on their faces.

"That was no security guard," Nancy said, her voice barely above a whisper. "That was Emily's rival, Peter Stine!"

14

Everything in Focus

Nancy and George remained frozen in the darkness, waiting until they were sure Stine was not going to pass them. Then Nancy said urgently, "Come on, George, let's see where he went." They moved out of the shadows. "Look!" Nancy whispered in George's ear.

Stine was standing in front of the huge sliding doors on the dock side of the warehouse. They watched him reach forward. A small door set into the sliding doors swung open, and Stine stepped quickly inside.

I should have realized that door was there, Nancy thought, even if I couldn't see it in the dark. She wondered about Stine. He'd opened the door as if he were confident it wouldn't be locked.

116

"He's been here before!" Nancy hissed as she tugged George's arm. The girls ran to the door but slowed as they neared it. Neither wanted to be heard by Stine.

The door opened readily with only slight pressure from Nancy. She was glad to find a few lights on in the warehouse, covering any light spilling from the street when she and George slipped through the door.

Inside, Nancy paused to get her bearings. She looked around the cavernous room filled with shelves and racks. The shelves were crammed with cardboard boxes, all neatly labeled. She moved closer. The labels were printed in an Asian language. The tall racks, arranged in a broad maze of aisles, were painted the same dull gray as the cold walls and distant ceiling.

Nancy scanned the room for Stine. "I wonder what this warehouse is for," she whispered to George. What products could possibly be part of the mystery that they were caught up in? Glancing at George, Nancy raised her eyebrows. "Where do you think Stine is?"

George, just as puzzled, shrugged her shoulders as she answered in a barely audible voice, "Who knows? I just hope we see him before he sees us!"

Nancy spotted an open box on a nearby shelf and stepped over for a closer look. The box was full of plastic bags, each holding tiny, thin boards with electronic circuitry printed on them. "George, look at this!"

But George was waving her over to another, larger box, filled with more plastic bags.

"Microchips!" George's voice was louder than she'd intended.

"Shh!" Nancy hissed. "Microchips and electronic circuitry," she whispered. "This warehouse is full of specialized computer parts!"

Nancy caught a flash of movement across the room. "There's Stine!" She pointed.

Peter Stine was threading his way silently through the room, zig-zagging from one aisle to the next as if it were all very familiar to him.

"Here goes," Nancy said.

Nancy and George followed Stine through the giant room, keeping a safe distance behind him. Stine reached a door marked "Boiler Room," opened it, and stepped inside, barely slowing his pace.

Nancy paused again. She heard a slight noise from inside the room, but she opened the door anyway. There was no sign of Stine. And no other door leading out of the room.

"Where could he have gone?" George whispered. One or two old, rusted tanks sat in the room. But there was no place for Stine to have hidden. "Nowhere!" Nancy said in puzzled frustration.

The girls cautiously began to explore the small space. A few moments later, Nancy pointed to a dim outline in the dust on the floor. Then she pointed to a recessed handle. It was a trapdoor.

Signaling George to move to one side, Nancy tested the handle. One gentle tug, and it moved easily. She raised the door.

A flight of stairs led down and into a dim passageway.

"I don't know, Nancy." George peered at the harshly lit passageway.

"It must be a secret tunnel," Nancy said in a low voice.

Stine was nowhere to be seen. Nancy listened for a moment for any noises in the tunnel. "I think we'd better follow Stine. If we don't, we might miss a chance to find Emily."

"You're right. I don't like the looks of that tunnel, though," George answered.

Nancy nodded in agreement, still listening intently. Hearing nothing from below, she swung her legs over the edge and lowered herself onto the steps. "Glad we're wearing jeans?" She grinned up at George.

The girls crept down the stairway. When they reached the bottom, they met a new challenge. They were faced with not just one underground tunnel but several. "Oh, great," Nancy sighed. There seemed to be no particular pattern to the way in which the dimly lit tunnels angled away from the corridor by the stairwell.

"This is like a maze, Nancy." George shook her head in dismay.

Nancy finally chose what looked like the main corridor, and she and George walked slowly along it, looking around at every step for Stine. But all was quiet, and they saw nothing.

"How could he have disappeared so fast? . . . Wait!" Nancy pointed toward another corridor. She could see light streaming through an open doorway at its end. "Let's try this way first."

The girls crept silently toward the doorway. They distinctly heard the sound of voices coming from the room beyond.

The room appeared to be large, although most of it was out of Nancy's line of sight. Gradually, she inched closer. Suddenly, a man paced by the doorway. Nancy recognized the balding head fringed with reddish hair. It was Arnie Blane, the thief who'd stolen Emily Foxworth's camera.

Blane's attention was focused on what he was saying so, fortunately, he didn't look out into the hallway. Instead, he turned to argue with someone in the room.

"Harold, you're nuts. Don't you understand? It's all off. The guy stiffed you, or he will soon. You've got to leave now!"

Blane paced back to the center of the room, while the voice of another man, deep and resonant, answered.

"What do you want me to do, Blane? Cut and run like a nervous kid? No. People know me."

Nancy inched still closer, huddling into a bend

in the tunnel wall, trying to get a look at the second man. What she saw made her blood freeze. The man was Harold Kesack, the one Emily thought was dead! His hair and beard were trimmed differently, but the Buddha on the chain around his neck was unmistakable.

Nancy discovered two small alcoves near the door that would let her move even closer to the room and still remain in the shadows. She crept into one, and George entered the other to scan the room from that angle.

Nancy hoped they would spot Emily in the room. But neither girl could see anyone, except Blane and Kesack, who Nancy assumed was Blane's boss. Kesack slumped wearily into a large armchair near the middle of the room. Blane continued to pace the floor anxiously.

George stepped back into the alcove to avoid being seen by Blane, and her foot kicked a small rock. The rasping sound was loud in the silent tunnel. She froze, but neither man seemed to have heard the noise.

"I'm telling you, Harold. You're not safe. Not here. We gotta get moving," Blane continued. "Anyway, I have to get something from storage." He left through a door at the back of the room.

Nancy waved to George, indicating that they should go back down the passageway. When they'd crept as far as the main corridor, Nancy stopped. "The police must be with Hannah by now," she whispered to George. "Let's go tell them we found Kesack."

But the girls hadn't taken more than a dozen steps toward the stairwell when loud footsteps echoed behind them, and Blane's voice stopped them.

Apparently, he had snaked through some connecting passages in order to cut off the intruders. "So it's you, is it?" He strode toward the girls and made sure that they saw the small revolver in his hand.

"Looking for your trouble-making pal Foxworth?" he snarled.

"Yes," Nancy answered.

"You won't find her here." Blane jerked his thumb toward the room where Kesack waited. The girls reluctantly returned through the passageway.

When they entered the room, Kesack stood up nervously. "Who are these two?" he demanded.

"Friends of Emily Foxworth," Blane spat back.

"What are you doing here? How did you get here? Who told you I was here?"

The man's rapid-fire questions told Nancy that he was angry—but, more than that, scared.

"Where's Emily?" she asked.

"I don't have her," Kesack snapped. But then he slumped wearily into the armchair again. While the girls stood under the watchful eyes of Blane, Kesack began to talk about Emily.

"She's good, you know. Fast with that camera of hers. Too fast sometimes. But honest. Her pictures were always true, not glamor stuff or exaggerated."

"She had some good shots of you," Nancy prompted him. To her relief, Kesack kept on talking.

"Toughest thing about planning my fake death five years ago was knowing that Foxworth might show up with her camera. She was smart. I thought the plane crash was the only thing that would work." He paused.

Nancy gave a slight nod, not wanting to stop the flood of words that might give her a clue to where Emily was.

"I'm sick of hiding, though," he went on. "You can't live when you have to stay hidden." Kesack seemed genuinely unhappy.

"What are you going to do, then?" Nancy asked.

"I'm going to strike a deal with the feds. I figure the government'll be fair with me if I talk, tell 'em what I know about all this." He waved his hands expansively, as if Nancy and George knew what the tunnels and warehouse were part of and would understand what he meant.

"So, what does Emily have to do with . . . all this?" Nancy waved her hands as Kesack had done.

"The mob. The mob. You know, I think they

suspected I wasn't dead. And then that woman shows up with her camera and starts taking pictures and gets some of me before I know it."

"Like the one of you getting off a fishing boat?" Nancy risked asking.

"Yeah. Exactly. Anyway, you can see I can't let pictures like that get around. The mob, they're looking for me. They see those pictures, I'm a dead man." Kesack leaned back in the chair, stretching for a moment. "But I didn't take Emily Foxworth. I just wanted those photos."

It was suddenly clear to Nancy that if Kesack hadn't kidnapped Emily and didn't know where she was, then things were worse than she thought. Kesack and Blane, George and herself, and Emily were all in great danger.

"Mr. Kesack, we've got to leave now. All of us. It's important. We're in serious danger here," said Nancy.

"Naw." The gangster stood up, confident again. "We're okay, kid. No one knows I'm here, except Croft."

"Why does he know?" Nancy asked quickly.

"He's the one got me back into the country. He's going to meet me here tonight, take me to a better hideout. You'll see. Kesack's going to land on his feet."

Nancy shook her head. "I don't think you're safe."

Kesack stared at her. "What're you doing here

in the tunnels, anyway?" he asked suddenly. "How did you get here?"

Producing the crumpled slip of paper from her jeans pocket, Nancy told Kesack about finding the number code. "I didn't figure it out until about an hour ago."

Kesack was clearly upset. "Where did you find that?" he roared.

"I, uh, lost it, chief." Blane looked uncomfortable. "It was Croft's code to tell us where to meet him tonight."

"I found it after Emily's apartment had been broken into the second time," Nancy volunteered.

"The second time?" Kesack repeated, alarmed.

"Yes. Someone tried to break in one night and failed. The break-in the next day was successful."

Nancy remembered the vandalism in Croft's Curio Shop. She turned to Kesack again. "Look, it must be the mob that has Emily now. And they broke into Croft's. Everything was torn up." Nancy looked steadily into Kesack's eyes. "They took some pages from a notebook that had handwriting like this in it. They might know you're here now."

"I was right, boss. See?" Blane jumped excitedly back from the doorway, where he had been nervously watching the tunnel passage. "What if they got Croft? We should get out of here now!"

125

The girls nodded in agreement. Kesack stood up suddenly. "Okay. I know these streets. Let's go." He turned to the girls, hesitating for a moment. Nancy knew he was trying to decide what to do with them.

But before he could make a decision, loud footsteps clattered down the tunnel. Obviously, more than one person was coming, and they didn't care who heard them as they charged toward the room where the girls and their captors stood.

Blane grabbed Kesack's shoulder and tried to shove him to the back door of the room. But as he did so, a slender man stepped silently from the shadows beyond the doorway. He was dressed in a dark suit, wore a small, dark hat, and held a pistol at his side. His other hand was tucked casually into a pocket.

Blane and Kesack stopped, confused. Nancy and George looked at each other and stood still. Nancy was sure that running would not do much for them or for Kesack. She turned to see who was coming down the tunnel. Maybe it would be the police or Hannah or even Peter Stine.

No. Nancy's earlier fears returned. Several men she had never seen before entered the room from the tunnel. With them were the two men who had chased her on the bridge. The crane operator looked grimly satisfied when he spotted Nancy.

"Why, hello, ladies," his companion said, sneering. "What are nice girls like you doing in a dump like this?"

The third man made Nancy uncomfortable. He was trim, dressed in an expensive suit. His eyes took in the room and its occupants with a confident, knowing sweep. But he said nothing.

The three men all leveled guns at Kesack, Blane, and the girls.

Should Nancy tell them the police were combing the docks this very minute? No, she wasn't sure Hannah had gotten through to Lieutenant Chin or been able to convince him of the importance of the code. It was a bluff that might not work.

"Well, if it isn't the dead chief." The voice of the third man, low and ironic, broke the silence. Nancy switched her gaze to Kesack, glad the attention of the mobster in the expensive suit was off her and George.

"Hello, guys." Kesack's nervously darting eyes belied his overconfident smile. "Glad to see the top guy back, after all?" He chuckled, but his laugh fell into the silence of the room and faded. No one joined him.

Arnie Blane shifted uncomfortably on his feet. He stepped away from Kesack. "I can explain—" he began uncertainly.

"Shut up." The snappily dressed man seemed to be the leader of the three, and he wasted no time on Blane. "Explanations are what I don't need. Not from you, not from him, not from anyone."

He took a few steps toward Kesack, and Nancy and George backed away.

"So, pictures don't lie." The crane operator chuckled as he watched the others. "I told you he was still alive."

The leader was within a few steps of Kesack. He stopped, still pointing his gun at Kesack's heart. "When you die, old man, you should stay dead," he said coolly. "Now you have to do it all over again. But this time"—he nodded at Nancy and George—"it won't be so lonely."

15

Burial at Sea

"Tie them up," the leader ordered the crane operator, throwing him a length of heavy rope. The crane operator grinned and proceeded to bind the hands of first Kesack and Blane, then Nancy and George.

"You almost got away with it, Kesack," the crane operator snarled. "But that's what we're here for—to prevent you from talking to the government. That was your plan, wasn't it?"

"You can't do this!" Nancy exclaimed, twisting her hands in a futile attempt to free herself from the ropes.

The crane operator turned to Nancy. "Too bad you got messed up in this, little lady." Then he looked at Kesack. "Really . . . too bad." He let out a low-pitched laugh that startled George.

She yelled at the top of her lungs. "Help!"

"No one's going to hear you down here, sweetheart."

"Gag them," the leader ordered. "We don't want anyone to notice our caravan outside."

One of the men placed a gag over Nancy's mouth and tied it securely at the back of her head. Then he gagged the other three. Blane protested, and for his efforts he was shoved heavily against the wall.

Kesack's eyes flamed in anger. "So Croft took off, did he? Well, no matter. We'll catch up with him sooner or later." He squirmed against the bonds that held him.

"It was Croft who gave you away, old man," the leader informed him. "We found notes in the curio shop that led us right to you. Come on," he directed his men. "Let's move them out of here."

Nancy found herself being shoved roughly down another branch of the tunnel, followed by George, Kesack, and Blane. Behind them were the rest of the mobsters.

No one will ever find us in here, she thought. Yet she held out hope that Hannah had reached Lieutenant Chin in time and that the police were now somewhere in the area, scouting around.

At that moment, Nancy realized something. She and George had followed Peter Stine into the warehouse, yet he was nowhere to be seen! And the thugs hadn't mentioned him. Where was he? And what was his role in the mystery?

A damp, rotting smell began to fill the air. Nancy had little time to contemplate Stine, since it was a struggle just to maintain her balance while walking with her hands bound behind her. The mobsters kept pushing their victims along, urging them forward. Nancy wondered where they were being taken.

After a good five minutes of winding through the underground tunnels, Nancy detected a whiff of fresh air. The distinct odor of the ocean wafted through the tunnel, and ahead she saw an opening.

The prisoners were led onto a rotting dock and held there until a launch approached. Nancy strained her ears, hoping to hear a police siren. She heard only the water lapping against the pier and the steady hum of the motorboat. She looked around for a way to escape, but, with her hands bound, the prospects seemed dim. Besides, the dock they stood on lay beyond large gates that most likely were locked.

Quickly, the four were loaded onto the launch. Nancy glanced at George. Real fear showed in her friend's eyes. Nancy, too, was worried, although she busied herself by trying to work her hands free and concentrating on a means of escape.

The captives were shoved below decks. Nancy kept her ears and eyes open. The steady hum of the motor and the gentle back-and-forth movement of the launch indicated to her that they were still on the bay. Once outside the breakwaters, the waves would be larger and the going quite rough.

Fifteen minutes later, the prisoners were ordered above decks and were loaded onto what looked to Nancy like an old fishing boat. She had little time to observe her surroundings, however, as she was pushed roughly along with the others deep into the interior of the boat.

"You can take their gags off," the leader indicated to the crane operator.

"Might as well let them share their last moments together, eh, boss?" The thin-faced man cackled cruelly. "No one can hear them out here, anyway." He untied the gags, making sure the prisoners' hands remained securely bound.

Then he led them down a narrow hallway and pointed to a door. "In there," he said gruffly. "We'll be back for you as soon as we get this old chug going and can make our way out to sea. Then it's time to feed the fishies." He laughed as he closed the door on them.

Nancy let her eyes adjust to the darkness. When she could see, she let out a surprised cry. "Emily!" she exclaimed. "Are you all right?"

"I'm okay. Really, Nancy," Emily assured her. "And am I ever glad to see a friendly face. I wish I could give you a hug." But Emily's hands, like those of the others, had been tied behind her.

"But I'm sorry you and George are here," she

added. "I'm afraid I got you into a real mess, girls," she said tearfully.

"I'll say," agreed another voice. Kesack's.

Emily's eyes widened. "You're supposed to be dead," she informed him.

The old man laughed bitterly. "I have the distinct feeling that I will be shortly."

"Well, your appearance here explains a lot of things."

"Like what?" George asked.

"Like why these thugs who've been holding me captive kept asking me what I knew about Kesack. 'Nothing,' I told them repeatedly, 'except that he died in a plane crash five years ago.' I guess they finally believed me."

"I wonder why they kept you, then," George said thoughtfully.

"Because," Nancy spoke up, "she was the perfect bait. When the mob discovered that Kesack was after Emily, they figured that all they had to do was kidnap her, and Kesack would walk right into their hands."

"Exactly," Emily said.

"Also," Nancy continued, "Emily gave them some protection from the police, especially Lieutenant Chin. The mob knew he was a good friend of Emily's and wouldn't allow anything to happen that might hurt her."

"But now that they have us," Blane said, gesturing to Kesack and himself, "I think we're *all* expendable."

"We've got to get out of here," Nancy said urgently. "Right now, before they get this boat started and make their way out to sea!"

While everyone was talking, Nancy had been attempting to remove the ropes that bound her hands. "George," she said to her friend, "turn around." George did as she was directed. Nancy backed into her. "These ropes are almost undone. They feel much looser. See if you can untie that last knot."

George tugged at the ropes for a good five minutes, and finally Nancy was free! She worked quickly to untie the others. "Emily," she whispered, "do you have any idea how many men are on board?"

"Not now," Emily answered. "But before you came . . . let's see, there were at least five. The cook, the guard, the three crew members . . . yes, at least five."

"Too many, then," said Kesack forlornly.

"Five, plus the crane operator—his pal, that thin guy with the gun—the leader, and there were a few others outside dressed like dockworkers," George said slowly.

"It's no good planning to take control of the boat," Nancy said. "We'll have to come up with another way." She thought for a moment. At last, she asked, "Can everybody swim?"

"Swim?" Kesack said. "You must be nuts. That water's freezing."

"I don't see that we have much choice," Nancy

told him. "Let's just hope we don't have to be in the bay too long." Secretly, Nancy wondered how Emily and Kesack would fare in the cold water. Blane looked strong enough, and she wasn't worried about athletic George, although swimming too long in the chilly Pacific waters would prove deadly for all of them.

"There's a guard stationed at the foot of the stairs," Emily cautioned.

Together, the group worked out a plan to overpower the guard.

Nancy repeated the plan to the others twice. "Are you *sure* you know what to do?" she kept asking them. "We can't afford to make any mistakes." She ran through the plan a third time.

"We know, we know," Kesack said irritably. He was used to giving orders, not taking them.

"All right, George," said Nancy. "You start things rolling. Call the guard in here. Yell to him that Emily needs medical attention."

"Okay," George said nervously. "I'll do my best." When the door was opened in response to George's cries, Blane knocked the burly guard unconscious. Kesack bound and gagged him, and then the prisoners quietly made their way to the top deck.

Silently, with Nancy in the lead, they crept to the bow of the boat. They had decided it would be easiest for them to scramble overboard from there. Emily, then George, then Blane and Kesack jumped over the side. Nancy was about to follow when she was spotted by one of the mobsters.

He shouted to the others, "They're getting away!"

Nancy heard a shot ring out. She ducked, momentarily deafened by the sound. Another shot rang out, and, without hesitating, she jumped overboard.

The icy water stunned her, and the salt burned her eyes.

"Nancy?" she heard George call. "Nancy, I can't find Emily!"

"I have her!" Kesack yelled.

Suddenly, the fishing boat and the surrounding water were illuminated by searchlights. Two police cruisers approached the fishing vessel, and a third searched the water for the swimmers. Nancy and the others were soon safely on deck, wrapped in wool blankets. Nancy felt someone thrust a cup of something hot into her hand.

From the safety of the police cruiser, she sipped hot coffee and watched the police officers board the fishing boat. There was a scuffle with the mobsters on deck, but no shots rang out.

"Hannah!" Emily suddenly cried out. Her teeth chattering uncontrollably, the soaked woman hugged her friend, both of them unmindful of the wet and cold.

Nancy and George smiled at each other, happy to see Hannah and Emily reunited. As they watched, the police handcuffed Kesack and

Blane and took them off to the lower deck, where they were secured in a temporary jail.

"I hope they consider the fact that he helped me in the water," Emily said of Kesack.

"Lieutenant Chin will take your statement into account, Emily," Nancy assured her.

In the excitement, Nancy was paying little heed to the continual flash of a camera from nearby. But after she'd warmed up and the shock had worn off, she realized that Peter Stine was capturing the entire event on film.

Shivering, she walked over to him. "Don't you ever quit?" she asked.

"Never," he replied.

Stine returned his attention to the commotion on the fishing vessel across the way. He snapped one picture after another of the capture. "For once," he said, "I've beaten Emily Foxworth out of a big story."

Emily chose that moment to join Nancy and George. Stine snapped a photo of his woeful-looking competitor. Then he let out a guffaw that rang in Nancy's ear long after they'd made their way safely to shore.

16

The Whole Picture

By the time Emily Foxworth and her guests woke the next day, the spring sunshine was pouring into Emily's apartment. They hadn't gotten to bed until almost dawn. After Nancy, Emily, and George had been rescued from the chilly waters of the bay, they'd been asked by the police to help sort out what had taken place. Along with Hannah, they had pieced together as much of the story as they could.

Although worn down by the strain of having been held prisoner by the mobsters, Emily had told the police everything about her kidnappers and her captivity. Then she listened, amazed, as Nancy and the others described the events that had taken place since her disappearance. The police, too, were impressed with the discoveries Nancy and her friends had made.

Nancy had been glad when Peter Stine had been forced by his paper's deadline to leave the wrap-up of the investigation. His glee at covering the story had made her very uncomfortable. It was as if Stine were glad that Emily had been in danger so that he could have a great story.

Finally, in the early-morning hours, the police had driven the four women to Emily's house. Emily didn't want to be alone, and no one felt like going to the hotel. While Tripod chattered joyfully, Emily and her guests had treated themselves to long, hot showers. Then they'd collapsed into bed for a much-needed sleep.

Emily, glad to be home, had risen first and started a hearty breakfast. Hannah entered the kitchen next, offering to help. "The smell of fresh coffee was all I needed to wake me up," she announced.

In a moment, George joined them, stretching. "Do I smell cocoa?" she said with a yawn. Nancy followed shortly after.

"See, Hannah?" Emily laughed. "Do I know how to recruit help in the kitchen?"

As George set the table, Nancy and Hannah made a fruit salad and omelets, and Emily kneaded the dough for sourdough biscuits.

After she had put the biscuits in the oven, Hannah took charge. "Everyone to the table now," she urged. "Sit down and start. I'll bring the biscuits when they're just right."

"You don't have to tell me twice," Emily agreed. She and the girls tackled the meal hungrily, and Hannah joined them soon with the biscuits.

Nancy asked Emily about her contacts in the underworld. "Kesack and Louie seem to respect you, Emily."

"Well, I think, in their own way, they see themselves as professionals, and they see me as a professional. And, although I've certainly never done business with Kesack, I think he knows I only tell the truth with my camera, and that can come in handy sometimes." Emily paused for a sip of coffee.

"What about Louie?" Nancy asked, reaching for a biscuit. "Did he help us somehow last night?"

Emily smiled. "Louie *did* help us. You're right, Nancy. He called earlier this morning to say goodbye."

"Goodbye, goodbye, goodbye!" Tripod's farewell made everyone laugh. The bird shuffled on his perch and preened his feathers contentedly.

"Why goodbye?" asked George, settling back in her chair with her cocoa.

"Was it Louie who called and told me to go to the bridge last night?" Nancy asked.

"Wait, I can't answer everything at once!"

Emily laughed. "One thing at a time. Louie is an informant I use sometimes."

Nancy nodded.

"He would periodically tell me of new developments he thought I'd be interested in. And he kept an eye out for me. He knew that sometimes the information he gave me put me in dangerous places with dangerous people."

"That's right," Nancy agreed. "He was trying to warn you before you were kidnapped." She grinned ruefully. "Only I think George and I scared him away the first night we were here, when we went for our walk."

"But Louie wasn't the one who called you about the bridge, Nancy," Emily went on. "He told me on the phone this morning that he would have tried to stop you from going. However, it *was* Louie who tipped off the police to look for you in the tunnels last night."

"I wonder how he knew?" Hannah asked, puzzled.

"Louie has his ways." Emily poured more coffee for Hannah. "He said he's 'going on vacation' for a while. When I asked him where, he'd only say that it was *far* away."

"I don't blame him. I wouldn't want those mobsters after me. Once was enough!" George took the last bite of a sourdough biscuit.

Nancy was still curious about being lured to the bridge. "Emily, if Louie didn't tell me to go to the bridge, then who did?"

"The men who tried to throw you off the bridge. They thought that you might have been in touch with Croft, and since they hadn't found him, they were afraid he might have told you too much."

The phone rang, and Emily answered it. Nancy and the others watched, half afraid there would be a new threat. But Emily smiled as she listened to the caller, and they relaxed. After a brief conversation, she hung up the phone and returned to her guests.

"Good news. Faith Arnold is much better now. It looks like she'll recover from her injuries."

Nancy and George exchanged relieved glances. Although they had distrusted the gallery owner at first, she had honestly seemed concerned about Emily.

"The gallery will be closed for a few weeks, until Faith is on her feet again," Emily went on, "but she's telling her visitors that she wants to extend the run of my exhibit."

"That *is* good news." Hannah smiled warmly. "You certainly deserve the attention."

"By the way, look what I found when I went downstairs to get the newspaper this morning," Emily said. She held out a large envelope, then opened it to reveal several photographs.

"The stolen pictures!" Nancy exclaimed. She recognized the prints that had hung on Emily's living-room wall, but not the others.

"These are the ones that were stolen from the gallery," Emily said, handing some pictures to Nancy. Kesack was in several of them, often just a figure in a shadow, but there nonetheless. The prints had been removed from their frames but had been handled carefully and were not any the worse for having been stolen.

"There was a little note from Harold Kesack, too. I guess he found a way to get someone to return these." Emily smiled.

"Will you keep working on 'Children of Change'?" Hannah asked worriedly.

"I certainly will!"

Nancy smiled as she saw the "old" Emily Foxworth again, full of life and energy.

Their conversation was interrupted by a light knock at the door. "It's Don Chin, Emily," a voice called softly. "Are you up yet?"

Because they were still comfortably gathered at the dining table, Emily pulled up a chair and offered the detective a cup of coffee, which he accepted readily.

"That is, I'll have some coffee if Emily is going to offer me one of her biscuits to go with it!" Everyone laughed as the lieutenant settled in his chair.

"Don, after all the work you've done for me the past few days, you can have a whole *batch* of biscuits if you want!"

"Don't give me *too* much credit, Emily. I

mean, sure, I worked hard, but I had a little help." He nodded to Nancy and George. "Anytime you two want to give me a hand with a case, you're welcome in San Francisco!"

"I'm glad George and I spotted Peter Stine going into that warehouse last night," Nancy said.

"Stine!" exclaimed Hannah angrily. "I think it was awfully unfair of him to take advantage of Emily's kidnapping so he could get a good story."

"I suppose he's going to say he scooped it," George added, "when Emily didn't even have a chance!"

"Well, I'm not so sure Stine has any edge over Emily." The lieutenant grinned and winked at Hannah as he reached for a second biscuit. "You see, the two stars of the story are Emily Foxworth and Harold Kesack."

Nancy watched Lieutenant Chin with interest. It was clear that he knew something that Emily and the others did not. And he was enjoying keeping them in suspense.

"What do you mean, Lieutenant?" Hannah asked.

Nancy took a guess. "Maybe he's trying to say that Stine will only get half the story."

"Almost right, Nancy. Stine *does* know better than to approach Emily for an interview, after the way he profited by her kidnapping."

"But you're thinking of something more, aren't you?" George was beginning to enjoy the lieutenant's guessing game.

"Oh, yes—I nearly forgot." With a wicked grin, he turned to Emily. "You're wanted down at the station as soon as possible."

"What?" Emily's surprise was reflected in the faces of her guests. This wasn't the pleasant mystery they had thought the detective was about to reveal.

"Well, it seems that our star criminal, Harold Kesack, is not only turning state's witness . . ." he began.

"Yes? Come on, Don!" urged Emily.

"He's also becoming quite selective about whom he's willing to speak with."

"What does that mean?" Hannah asked.

"It means, my friends, that Kesack is refusing to grant interviews. He'll have nothing to do with the press."

"Oh." Emily's disappointment was clear.

"He has particularly asked that a photojournalist named Peter Stine be barred from taking his picture or, for that matter, from being present at any interviews or questioning sessions."

"Good!" cried George and Hannah together.

"However?" Nancy prompted him, sensing that the officer still had news to reveal.

"However, Kesack has made one request."

"Which is?"

"Which is that he be allowed an exclusive set of interviews with one journalist—Emily Foxworth. Kesack will speak to no one else."

There was a moment of silence before Emily reacted to the news, and her friends broke into excited cheers.

"Well," said Emily, after draining her coffee cup, "if you'll excuse me, I think I'd better put some film in my cameras and head for the police station!" She stood up and walked toward the darkroom.

"By the way, Nancy," the lieutenant continued, "don't give Stine too much credit for being crafty. He wouldn't have found the tunnels if he hadn't seen Blane going down there a few days ago. He recognized Arnie Blane from one of Emily's photos and followed him."

"So he knew about Kesack?" Nancy asked.

"Yes. It appears he knew for several days before everything began happening."

"Shouldn't he have tipped the police off?" Nancy wanted to know.

"As a matter of fact, he should have," agreed Lieutenant Chin, "and that's been brought to his attention. He received a severe reprimand from the police department and from his boss at the newspaper, and he's likely to get a stiff fine if the D.A. decides to prosecute. His actions during this case have been highly unprofessional."

"I'll say," George agreed.

"We've impounded the warehouse and the

computer parts in it," the lieutenant went on. "It seems Croft was smuggling more than just Harold Kesack in and out of the country. He won't have any profit this time. We're confiscating everything until the investigation is complete."

"Well, all's well that ends well, right?" Hannah set down her coffee cup and surveyed the remains of their leisurely breakfast. She smiled at Nancy and George, then at Don Chin.

"What will you be doing for the rest of your holiday?" the lieutenant asked them.

Emily called to them from the darkroom. "I promised not to get all caught up in my work while you were here. I think I failed!"

"Miserably." Hannah tried to sound grumpy and disappointed but wasn't convincing.

"Well, I promise you, I'll wrap up my interview with Kesack in plenty of time to meet you tonight at any restaurant you want."

"It's a deal!" Hannah exclaimed.

Nancy, George, and Hannah all began talking at once about where they wanted to go.

"Hey, today is four-twelve," George announced.

"Oh, no, not another number mystery," Nancy groaned.

"No. It means we've still got three days of vacation left! I vote we make the most of it."

Emily emerged from the darkroom, carrying a bulging bag of camera gear. "Well, then, what would you like to see?" she asked.

Hannah wrinkled her forehead as she cleared off the table. "In all the excitement, I haven't had time to think about it."

Nancy looked out the window at the sparkling bay. It was a brilliant, clear day. Suddenly, she giggled.

"What do you want to see, Nancy?" Emily asked.

Nancy looked mischievously around the table at her friends. "I was thinking another boat ride might be fun."

"A boat ride?" Hannah asked, confused.

"Yes." Nancy stood up and pointed out the window. "What about a trip to that little island in the bay?" she suggested.

Hannah stood up, too. "What little island?" she asked.

Nancy looked at her and giggled again.

"Alcatraz Island, Hannah, where all the bad guys used to live."